Editor: Jacques Bakke
Book Designer: Amy Harris
[illegible]: Tori McGowan
Copyright [illegible] Publisher
Back Cover Art [illegible] Photographer: Amber D. Smith

April 16, 2025 - August 7, 2025
Fort Rincon [illegible] Mesa Inc, NY, Cast Bronze 3772,
[illegible] 40" / West Point KS

[illegible] narrated by Brian Pierce
[illegible] written by Harry Carpenter
[illegible] Companion [illegible] documentary [illegible]
[illegible] 24 years

[illegible] Original Artwork drawn by [illegible] winter, [illegible] published
[illegible] Will Report Legal, John F. Boyle & Charles [illegible]
(Index)

Editor: Denise Barker
Graphic Designer: Amy Hunter
Formatter: Kari Holloway
Copywriter: Gerri Rodriguez
Back Cover Author Photographer: Marissa D'Angelo

Copyright 2025

April 16, 2025 – August 9, 2025
Fort Belvoir, VA / Alexandria, VA / Glen Burnie, MD /
Fort Meade, MD / West Point, KY

The novelization written by Brian Paone
Crew interview answers written by Harry Carpenter
Chapter 11 catering company interview answers written by
Marissa D'Angelo
Chapter 13 composer interview answers written by the band
members of Hiphopmcdougal: Julian Biggs & Charlie
Hodgson

OPENING CREDITS

A FOREWORD BY
AUTHOR HARRY CARPENTER

When I learned that my best friend, Brian Paone, had landed the incredible opportunity to novelize my most beloved underground film of all—a dream project for any writer—I immediately knew I needed to be involved. The excitement was electric! I started to explain the significance of his involvement, my voice catching slightly as I addressed him as both friend and another fan of the original movie; we then mutually agreed that my perspective should open the discussion.

I was too young to see the movie during its brief theatrical release. My dad was into old slashers and B-movies that would constantly play at the local drive-ins and historic theaters, and the opportunity came up during a double-feature night. The deal was sealed, and a sense of anticipation washed over me, leaving me eager for what was to come. As they say, the rest is history.

Remembering my first night seeing it, I knew my dad had taken off work that afternoon. He loved his job, building various woodworked household essentials, like cabinets and stairs. He sped home so fast that there wasn't a speck of sawdust on the man. I remember his excitement as he burst through the door to tell me we were doing a 7:00 p.m. showing of a movie he absolutely loved from ten years ago.

I was seven at the time, and the early '90s were plagued with films trying to live up to the hype of the previous decade. The '80s was a revolutionary time for slashers, monsters, and overall thriller-horror movies. We watched on repeat more times than I could count films like *Big Trouble in Little China*, *Ghostbusters*, and his personal favorite, *The Toxic Avenger*. I'd grown up on these films. The level of excitement at seeing them never dissipated for my dad, and seeing the joy in his expression as he showed me the printed tickets in his hand solidified the deal on the experience we would have that night.

I vividly remember the evening. We started off by having a wonderful meal at a local Mexican joint, Two Amigos. My dad kept making the joke of asking where the third one was. I was too young at the time to draw the correlation between his joke and the Steve Martin film. I had my usual plain taco plate from the children's menu, and we knew the rest of the night would push the bar higher and higher.

We went to this old theater in town called the Senator. The theater still stands today, its marquee glowing with the titles of both classic and modern films, inviting moviegoers inside. If you're looking for an authentic old-timey movie experience, this is your spot; the theater's aged yet comforting atmosphere is unparalleled. A faded vintage-style marquee sign, its lights buzzing softly, greeted us as we approached the entrance, showcasing the evening's film selection. At the time, I remember one or two names on the list. I remember there being *Fried Green Tomatoes*, which, to this day, I still have yet to watch. The other movie was a sequel to *Teenage Mutant Ninja Turtles*, which I felt bad for wanting to see instead.

Inside, a cavalcade of patrons came and went in the tight corridors. My dad pointed at the concession stand and told me that I could get one candy and one popcorn. I waited eagerly in line for my turn to pick. The lady behind the counter was some brunette girl, with a large beret hat. I remember the hat. I also recall that they were out of half the candy I liked, and so I opted for Raisinets, which, at the time, were my least-favorite candy.

Dad took my hand and carried an armful of our score to the theater. The screening room was all the way down this long hallway. It smelled of popcorn butter and a scent I can only describe as "old." It wasn't unpleasant. If I had to describe it now, it would be similar to a fragrance you would find in a historic landmark house or maybe an old library. Just a vintage smell. Hard to describe or place but, when you smell it, you know it.

Our screening room was fairly packed. It seemed my dad wasn't the only one who was hyped for his favorite movie returning to the big screen for a ten-year anniversary. I didn't know what I was getting into, but I knew he had good taste, even in bad movies. We quickly found empty seats midway up the aisle and settled in.

There were no previews. The movie launched with the traditional splash screens of the production houses, and we were kicking off. The first flood of credits of the cast and directors hit. Crickets chirped. Nothing was on the screen yet. Just words. As a kid, this could have filled me with anticipation or broken the mood. Eagerly I waited. If my dad said it was good, by God, it was. And then the opening theme kicked on.

For the next hour and twenty minutes, I sat glued to my seat. I don't know whether I even finished my Raisinets. I was in a trancelike state. The characters. The special effects. A ton of dialogue that went over my young head. This was the movie of movies. I left the theater that night a changed boy.

I never got to properly thank my father for taking me to his favorite stupid movie. He's fine with that. Yet, as of the writing of this, I hope he knows how impactful the movies he shared with me changed who I became. So, I guess we can consider this block of text to be my official *Thank you* to him. Sincerely, without the library of films my father introduced me to, I wouldn't be the writer I am today.

After this experience, I remember being in middle school a few years later. Several of my friends were sitting in my art class, discussing a new movie that had dropped. *American Werewolf in Paris* had just hit the theaters, and my friends couldn't stop talking about it. I felt my expertise was required. I let them know about the original *American Werewolf in London* version, which is far superior. This sparked a debate about films and, ultimately, about werewolf films.

I don't know how long this discussion lasted, but we took it to several other classes and, eventually, continued it on the walk home. I felt like I had found my moment to interject, with my ace card up my sleeve. During one dramatic pause to fish for a thought, I interrupted my friend Joe and belted out the name of my father's beloved film.

"Never heard of it. Is it like *American Werewolf in Paris?*" Marcus asked.

With a careless shrug, I let my arms fall to my sides. I hadn't actually seen the *Paris* sequel because something about it felt gimmicky and forced. The original was a classic. I tried to explain it was nothing like that. It was more visceral. This one was good. A classic from the '80s. I didn't need to explain any further. The three of us knew what the plan was on Friday night after school. We would have a movie night at Marcus's house.

Blockbuster, for a fact, didn't have the movie. I'd wandered the aisles a dozen times trying to rent a Sega game, while my mom viewed the latest releases. I would always tiptoe to the R-rated area and scope out the films. So many classics graced their shelves, but they were always the popular classics, like *Halloween* or *A Nightmare on Elm Street*. I could never find *my* movie.

I begged my mom to take me and Joe (who had decided to tag team the situation to ensure the acquisition of the film) to Bill's Video Emporium, right off the main highway. Mom never liked that place because of their dirty movie corner with the curtain. After a lot of arm twisting, she obliged.

Joe and I rushed right to the horror section. No hiding it from her this time. We outnumbered her, and we were grown! We were easily fourteen! Practically adults! The two of us ran through the alphabet to find our film of choice for the evening.

I ran my hands along the selection, reading the different titles. I saw *Amityville Horror*, and even *Aliens* was in the mix. While great, this was not the film of choice for the evening. Finally, after going to the next rack, I found it. Just past *Halloween 1-5*, almost glowing, it called to me. The title font looked like claw marks, and a foreboding wolf graced the cover. This was the film. This was it.

I brandished it and held it out to Joe, who stared at it, puzzled. He'd never seen this film before. In keeping with the monster theme, we also grabbed a copy of *Blade* to start the night right. Marcus's dad had no issue with us watching superhero movies. We figured we'd start with that until it was late enough to shift gears. It was the ultimate plan.

I quickly tracked down my mother, and she checked out our films. The guy behind the counter gave a puzzled look as he showed it to his coworker. He held up my movie. *The* movie. Immediately the guy leaned over the counter for a high five.

"Right on, little dude!" said the frosted-tipped coworker. Clearly he had seen the movie too.

Joe took notice, and that changed his opinion. He was now far more excited than he'd been in the past. Movie night tonight would be absolutely killer.

My mom dropped us off at Marcus's house around 6:00 p.m. His dad was cooking on the grill, and everyone else was already in the pool. Joe quickly dropped his bags, retrieved his swim trunks, and with Wonder Woman–spinning speed, he was changed and diving into the pool. I just wanted to start this film!

After about a dozen Marco Polo games and a game we called Lifeguard—which, looking back, was dangerous because you played a Fire Marshall Bill–type character, rushing to your friend. We would yell, "I'll save you!" and dunk them under water, screaming, "Breathe!" each time we dunked them. In hindsight, what a stupid game. At the time, it was the most fun I had ever had.

We gorged ourselves on hotdogs, grilled corn, and the biggest frigging burger you'd ever seen. Marcus's dad could give a masterclass on cooking. I had nearly forgotten about my coveted movie. After eating, our friends Devin and John joined the party. They'd missed the pool and dinner but tagged in for some N64, which Marcus had owned since the release. Again, this just furthered the distractions from my movie.

Finally, around 9:00 p.m., we popped in *Blade*. It's not a terrible vampire movie based on a superhero, but it wasn't the movie I wanted. Sure, it was bloody. It wasn't my movie. I patiently waited through a slew of swords, puns, and vampires, until the credits rolled. I don't think his blade finished swinging before I cut off the tape. Prodigy, or whatever techno music played, barely formulated a beat before the tape flew out.

"Dude!" Marcus yelled.

I didn't care. I quickly fished for the clamshell that contained my other movie, haphazardly tossing aside *Blade*, tape safety be damned. It was getting late, and I didn't want anyone to doze off. I checked the tape to ensure the previous renter had given it a proper rewind. I didn't want to wreck the experience by starting mid-film or at the end credits.

As the VCR autotracked, I knew we were in for a treat. I pressed the Volume button a handful of times, as this was two or three years before Marcus's dad upgraded the basement to the ultimate man cave, with the Bose sound system. We made do on the twenty-seven-inch tube TV. I hurriedly took my seat, and Marcus cut the lights. It was time.

"So, what is this movie about?" John asked.

I quickly shushed him.

The advertisements kicked on. I hadn't experienced previews in the theater. I had to see some coming-soon-to-own-on-home-video films, which had been out for the better part of half a decade at this point. Nothing but a few indie films that had gone straight to video. Five film trailers felt like an eternity.

Then the screen darkened. It was silent, save for crickets chirping. The names splashed across the screen, then faded. It was so plain. I knew if we made it to the opening scene, we would be set. Marcus was already losing interest, and Joe was adjusting his position. John was curious about the film, and Devin was already poised to go to sleep. Another few splash screens of credits and these guys would be sitting in front of the television, glued for the next hour and a half.

Then the opening theme kicked in. Much like I felt a few years ago, I think something clicked with them too. I saw Marcus paying attention. Joe couldn't look away. Hell, even Devin woke up to watch. He remained in his sleeping bag, his head cocked upward to watch for the next ten or fifteen minutes, before he adjusted his position. I don't think anyone said a word. Just jaw-dropping fun.

By the time we hit the hand-to-paw combat scene at the end, I knew we were locked in for this as the greatest movie of all time. When it was over, the credits rolled, and a hush fell over the room. I didn't know how to react to them. Did they like it? Did they absolutely hate it?

"*Duuuuude*!" Joe yelled as he stood.

Marcus quickly rose to his feet as well. "Especially the part with the Uzi! Holy shit!" He quickly clapped his hand to his mouth and looked up the stairs. I don't think his parents heard.

"What about the guy named Joey?" Joe asked.

Clearly he was taken by the fact that a character shared his name. It's always fun to hear your name in a movie as a kid. Marcus and Joe tried to recreate the fight scene, Joe brandishing his claws, while Marcus tried to find anything in his dad's workout room to use as a weapon. He ultimately settled on a jump rope. The rest of us were entertained by an even-lower-budget version of the best fight scene of all time. Some of my best childhood memories centered around screenings of this film.

It wasn't until I was in the army—many more years later—that I got the opportunity to show the movie to a new group of unsuspecting victims. I remember we were all gathered in the dayroom—a common room that everyone used, containing sofas, chairs, a television, and basic entertainment necessities. We had a DVD player, an Xbox 360, and a mini-fridge that we all split the cost on to add to the room. We were there for a long-enough time, so why not make the best of it?

I happened to mention to PFC Ammerman and Sgt Ullrich that I had a movie on DVD that everyone just had to see. I got a raised eyebrow from them, and we decided that on Saturday, when the gang all got together, we would watch this "disaster of a film," as Ammerman put it. His words, not mine. It was a masterpiece. I think my pitch of a B-movie equates to being terrible to him. He was about to learn something on Saturday.

We ran laps. We trained. We sweated. Monday to Friday, we did our jobs. Finally, on Saturday, the day had finally come. A few of us packed into SPC Grover's Jeep and went to the local PX, which was like a military 7-Eleven. We snagged bagfuls of snacks, beers, and the usual trappings of a movie night and bolted back to the common room.

The sun hadn't quite set yet, and a disgusting glare always whitewashed the television from about 1700 to 1930 hours, so we wanted to have the best possible viewing experience. We called Domino's and eagerly awaited the delivery, while several others played Guitar Hero. It was a packed room, including several who we knew but were not in our immediate circle. We turned on the television and watched a few reruns of *People's Court*, which was airing for some reason at this hour.

Ammerman collected the pizza from the barracks' front desk downstairs. It was time. The sun had just passed over the mountain, and we closed the thinly veiled curtain to obscure the remaining light. The television's glow of *People's Court* would be our only light, if only momentarily. I withdrew the disk from the case and slid it into the DVD player. I never enjoyed using the Xbox because sometimes it would overheat badly.

I think I hated the DVD for one reason and one reason only: the menu. The theatrical version and the VHS both kind of jumped right into the credits and cued the theme song, and the movie was off. A bit of something was lost at the looping theme song during the menu, as I could choose Play, Chapters, or Extras. It would have been cool if these guys added behind-the-scenes footage, but the DVD extras only included the trailer and an even lower-budget music video for the movie's theme song, written and performed by Hiphopmcdougal. Bummer.

However, speaking of the band who wrote the score, the year my father took me to the tenth anniversary rerelease in the theater, I only asked for two things for Christmas: the soundtrack's expanded deluxe two-disk box set and REO Speedwagon's *Wheels Are Turnin'* on CD. Let's just say that Christmas 1996 was one for the ages.

Back to movie night in the barracks, I quickly pressed Play to not ruin the ambiance of the opening. With the volume cranked to eleven, I sat in a folding chair to the left of the room to have a good view of the film and of everyone's reactions. As was tradition, the crickets chirped. The credits came and went. Then the Hiphopmcdougal-penned theme song hit. It was like a grenade had gone off. I never heard more whooping and hollering from grown men in all my life.

Almost ninety minutes later, as the film neared its close, laughter and excitement filled the room. At least one of us could not breathe because of a joke used in the film. It was a funny line about a fork but not that funny. Maybe I had been too young to get it at the time, and now it was not funny because I'd heard it so much? Either way, I was delighted to know it was a hit.

Then we deployed. Unfortunately, some of us didn't come home. The silver lining (get what I did there? Silver?) is that I still occasionally get a text from Ammerman or Grover to say they saw the movie on a streaming service or something, and it made them think of me. Ullrich hit me up a few months ago to ask if I'd seen that they were remastering the film to Blu-ray and digital download. It's nice to know they're all thinking of me when an article mentions the film.

That brings me full circle to why I needed to express all that. Sure, it was anecdotal, taking my stories at face value, but I can tell you that my experiences were all pleasant ones—from watching with my father on the big screen years ago, to forcing my childhood friends to experience it with me during our formative years, to sharing it with brothers-in-arms to shake the pre-deployment jitters. This movie has been a major part of my life, alongside other cult classics. It will always have a place in my home.

I can't begin to express the gratitude I have to the filmmakers, actors, and even Brian for writing this fantastic novelization. He is the only other guy I've met who organically liked the movie. Amid his love of time travel and DeLoreans, a cheesy horror from the '80s is up there on his list of interests. I know, with him, we're in for a faithful re-creation of the script.

While I couldn't be involved in the actual writing process, I advised Brian on numerous occasions, while he was scribing the book, to feel free to bounce ideas off me. Who better than, dare I say, the number-one fan of this film? Even if Brian hadn't allowed me to write this introduction, you best believe I would have a copy of the finished book up there alongside the VHS, DVD, Blu-ray, and even the LaserDisc and the film score on 8-track that I managed to track down on eBay a few years ago. I'm actually awaiting my order for the Japanese movie poster in the mail, so I hope that goes well. Maybe I'll take a photo of my collection and share it with Brian to take around with the books? Who knows?

In any case, I truly hope I am not the only one who experienced an entire lifetime of this film molding their life. I tell people that this movie and *Mortal Kombat* are the only for-sure things in my life. It's my equivalent to the death-and-taxes joke. It sounds a bit obsessive, but a fan will be a fan, right? I don't know whether I would be this over the moon if it wasn't so impactful in my life.

From my childhood, attending a bigger-than-life screening, to watching a digital copy on my phone while I ride on a plane to somewhere, I can't stop. It all stems to a double-feature movie night, where I don't even recall what the other feature was. That's how powerful this movie is to me. I can't describe it, much like some people are with sports or maybe even music. It's a movie, yes. But, to me, it's more than that.

I don't speak much to the friends I made in grade school, but I'm sure some of them are tormenting their families with this cheesy movie from before we were born. I would like to think so anyway. The reality is likely that this movie didn't impact them the same way and that they've moved on. It's nice to dream though, right?

As for a theatrical run, I'm hoping this book generates enough hype for a rerelease of the film in theaters. While 1986 was a long time ago, it doesn't stop places from showing a movie again. Maybe we can hope for a forty-eight-year anniversary soon? Time can only tell.

Some key scenes still play vividly in my mind. I particularly remember bits of dialogue, including some in-jokes about silverware. The scene with the zoo sticks in my mind as one of the most visceral and entertaining ones in the film. Then again, who can forget the *They Live*-esque fight scene at the end? Man and beast squaring off for an ultimate showdown? Chef's kiss, for sure.

One thing is for certain. I am not the world's expert on horror movies, but I know a good one when I see it. I'm dying with anticipation to read this novel all about our favorite 1980s' classic. More than enough stories exist about vampires (Lord knows that's true) and a heaping helping of monster stories. And, in recent years, movies and books have been coming out about werewolves.

Let's clear the air. I adore all those stories, from the hordes of relentless zombies to the unnervingly vicious killer albatross, but this film possesses a captivating *je ne sais quoi*. Words fail to capture its essence—the sight, the sounds, the overall feeling; you must experience it firsthand. I'm sure the book will be great, but trust me, the movie—with its gripping score and intense visuals—is something special. Snag the physical media. Don't miss out on the soundtrack; it brings the whole experience to life.

There's not a part of this movie that isn't good. I think that's due in part to the fact that this isn't a story about werewolves. It's a story about something worse than werewolves.

We're dealing with…

HOWLERS

CHAPTER 1
ATTACK AT THE ZOO

Heels *clack* loudly on the sidewalk. The darkness of night shrouds a row of trees to Brenda's right. She hefts her pocketbook farther on the shoulder of her yellow blouse as her blond ponytail sways with each bounce of her step. She scans the area ahead of her for any movement. The news reports from the past month of residents going missing, never to be heard from again, has become Talbotsville's personal epidemic.

Brenda wonders why none of the surrounding towns have had the same affliction brought upon them. She shakes her head to stop herself from falling down that rabbit hole—a rabbit hole full of conspiracy theories that only lead to fear.

And Brenda knows, if she could just clear this row of trees, she will be in the zoo's well-lit parking area. She thought accepting an extra shift tonight at the zoo would have been cathartic. Something she needed to tune herself out and to get her mind off… *him*. Feeding the elephants and giraffes and cleaning their enclosures *had* made her feel better, albeit for a short time. But here she is, huffing toward her car in the employee section—the most distant parking lot from the zoo's entrance. The chirping of bats deep in the woods to her right mixes with the sound of her heels *clack, clack, clack*ing on the pavement with each stride, alongside the cacophony of sounds from the animals penned inside the zoo.

Brenda's breath hitches in her throat when she hears rustling from the leaves just ahead of her. She wrings her hands, looking behind her, and hopes a car of exiting zoo-goers will pass—so its headlights can illuminate the dark woods and can show her how her imagination is getting the best of her. Whatever killer is stalking the Talbotsville streets certainly isn't hiding in the tree line at the edge of the sidewalk from the zoo entrance to the parking lot, right? And certainly the killer won't be interested in someone like little ole her, right?

No cars. No headlights to help brighten her path. The streetlamps not only are useless but seem to make focusing on the pathway harder, as the shadows seem… darker in between the showers of light.

The *clack, clack, clack*ing of her heels quickens now as Brenda breaks into a full powerwalk. The hairs on the back of her neck rise as she glances behind her one last time, hoping for any sort of vehicle to brighten the tree line.

Brenda holds her breath, thinking that minimizing any sound might deter the faceless killer of Talbotsville from pinpointing her location on the pathway. The neon Employee Parking sign slowly becomes visible ahead. That becomes her destination. That becomes her haven, where she can find solace in her vehicle and can drive home.

If she had only accepted her boyfriend's offer to drive her to and from work tonight. Then she could go directly to his house for his terribly made and overly greasy tacos. Yet a terrible and greasy taco sounds like heaven right now, especially compared to the deafening silence of the woods to her right—silence because she notices all sounds from the zoo and from within the woods have ceased. Did something scare them? Did they see something that spooked them? *Sensed* something maybe?

Silence continues until the leaves rustle again, now almost directly next to her.

A towering and broad silhouette leaps from the tree line and squares off in front of Brenda on the sidewalk. A squeal sticks inside Brenda's throat as her heart explodes with fear and adrenaline. The figure, shadowed by the streetlight behind it, lunges forward, growling.

Brenda stumbles backward and, with one fluid motion, slides her pocketbook off her shoulder and swings it at the Talbotsville Killer, striking him in the shoulder. Her eyes widen, and her stomach does Olympic-worthy summersaults as a furry paw swats away her bag and reaches for her throat. The confusion and shock of seeing a threadbare and tattered outfit on something crytpid makes her pause just long enough for the Talbotsville Killer—or *creature?*—to grab her pocketbook strap.

The Talbotsville Creature growls again—a deep guttery growl, one so inhuman that Brenda thinks, if she survives this attack, she may never get that sound from between her ears. Yet the spittle from its maw draws Brenda from her reverie.

She plants her feet and takes another, more violent and concise swing of her pocketbook at the killer's face. The creature raises its furry arms in defense and cocks its head to the side, exposing all its glory into the cone of the light from the streetlamp.

Brenda, stunned and trying to take it all in, screams and swings her pocketbook once more. Even while she does that on what feels like autopilot, she beholds every inch of this creature. Its pointed and furry ears sharpen into focus. Its crimson-stained razor-sharp teeth are chomping and drooling, soaking its hair-covered chin. Her screams and swings of her bag fade somewhere into the distance as the creature tries to navigate through the onslaught of her bag as she swings, swings, swings at its face.

But those eyes. The eyes captivate Brenda. The eyes deflate her fear. The eyes remove her will to fight. To escape. The eyes speak to her. The eyes tell her to…

Brenda screams longer than she thinks her lungs can even hold air, right as the creature's knifelike teeth sink into the soft flesh of her neck. She grips the creature's shoulders and feels the fabric of its flannel shirt. All her fight drains from her with each chomp to her carotid artery.

Numbness overtakes her, and her fingers tingle too much to feel the creature's ripped shirt anymore. Brenda is unsure if she is even still touching the creature's shoulders at all. She doesn't notice when her pocketbook slumps from her hand and crumples onto the sidewalk.

Then darkness comes… and the sound of her heels scraping over the pavement toward the tree line as the Talbotsville Killer drags Brenda into the sanctity of the woods, where he can feed. And where she will become more than meets the eye.

But with one final burst of survival reflex, Brenda kicks her high heel into the creature's eye and uses the fleeting frozen moment—when the creature's paw clamps over its face—to crawl from the tree line, her vision graffitied with dots of blackness that expand with every inhale. Through the swirls of darkness invading her eyesight, she discerns her discarded pocketbook lying on the pavement.

Brenda reaches for it. And then the darkness consumes her, her body failing her. The pool of blood forming under her neck slowly accomplishes what Brenda's hand could not do.

It touches the strap of her black pocketbook.

The next day, the sun rises on the sleepy inhabitants of Talbotsville, with the horrors that befell the town during the late evening hours unknown to them.

Brothers Joey and Brad Bradshaw traverse Western Avenue, a black Nikon camera slung around Joey's neck that he spent all summer before his senior year saving up to buy. The slight breeze blows Joey's long unkempt hair to the side while he switches out the camera lens.

A siren wails in the distance, from a police car or maybe from an ambulance. Joey doesn't know which it is; he was always terrible at matching the siren sounds with their emergency vehicles. As kids, Brad teased Joey whenever they played with their Matchbox cars because Joey would make a *woo-woo-woo* sound as he zipped the toy firetruck around the couch cushions. Even as a college student now, Joey still heard his older brother's teasing: *"Joey, you're so dumb. Everyone knows that's not what a firetruck sounds like. Sheesh."* Young Joey would run to cry to their mother, who settled the argument by putting the Matchbox cars on a "time out" and making the brothers do something productive with their time, like memorize the state capitals or the order of the American Presidents.

The brothers haven't seen each other since Joey came home for Christmas break last year. So, while Brad waits for Joey to finish securing the camera lens, he asks, "What have you been up to?"

"Just working at my internship at the local newspaper near my university." Joey adjusts his thick-framed black glasses on his nose.

"Yeah? How's that been going?" Brad runs his hand over his close-shaven head. The wind whips open his unbuttoned shirt, exposing a white tee-shirt underneath.

"It's going okay, but the editor thinks I need to take more initiative."

Brad furrows his brows and places his palms outward, as if to say, *How hard could that be?*

Joey notices his brother's reaction as they walk. "Well, how am I supposed to do that when nothing ever happens in this town?" Then, to drive home his point, he adds, "Welcome to Talbotsville, USA. Population: *boring*."

"C'mon, lil bro. You'll catch your big scoop soon."

"Thanks, big bro." Joey smiles and lovingly pats Brad's shoulder. "So anyway, how are you and Barbara?"

"Barbara? *Um*, pretty good." Brad's eyes alight when he spots someone walking toward them from a driveway. "There she is now."

Barbara strolls toward the brothers, an identical blond ponytail, like her twin sister Brenda's, bobbing with each step. "Hey, guys." She waves at the brothers and smiles at Joey.

"Hey, Barbara. How are you doin'?" Joey asks as Brad scoops up his girlfriend in a hug.

When Barbara breaks free from Brad's embrace, she says, "Good. How are you doing?"

"Pretty good." Joey raises his camera to chin level and shakes it slightly to punctuate his next sentence. "Well, I gotta go take some pictures. I'll see ya guys later."

Barbara waves and says goodbye as Joey trots away from them and farther down the street.

"All right. Bye, Joey," Brad calls out sarcastically, with a scoff and a chortle, and shakes his head, perturbed that his brother would vamoose so quickly after just meeting up from so many months of not seeing each other. "He's been working so hard," Brad explains to Barbara. "My little brother is growing so fast."

"He really is. Look at him." They watch Joey stop about thirty yards ahead to take a quick shot of a discarded leash on someone's front lawn—a dog nowhere in sight.

"Yeah," Brad agrees but can't help the feeling that the divide among the brothers is just growing wider with each passing year—Joey really throwing himself headfirst into his passion for photography at a faraway college, and Brad doing... well, *Brad things* in their hometown. He suppresses the feelings of nostalgia as quickly as he can, not allowing himself to fall down that slippery slope; sometimes there is no coming back from that. Brad forces himself from his thoughts to smile at Barbara. "So, how's your day been going?"

Barbara shrugs. "I still haven't heard from Brenda."

"What? What do you mean?"

"She went to work at the zoo yesterday, and we haven't heard from her since, so... It's been all night, and nobody knows where she is."

"My God."

"I know!"

"Wow. It's gonna be okay." Brad flashes Barbara one of his debonaire smiles and hugs his girlfriend again.

"I hope so," Barbara answers, her voice muffled in Brad's flannel shirt from the embrace.

Brian Paone: We are here with Juan O'Malley, Director of Photography.

Juan O'Malley: It's pronounced, *One* O'Malley.

BP: Thank you for correcting me. How difficult was it to shoot 90 percent of the movie at nighttime?

JO'M: Shooting at night presents unique challenges, but—for an expert in locations and angles, such as myself—we saw no issues. The real trick was to find lighting to represent natural daylight in utter darkness, which takes the eye of a genius.

BP: What were some of your previous works that made you the quintessential top expert in camera angles?

JO'M: Prior to *Howlers*, I worked on such prestigious films as *Pitch Dark*, *Cave Dwellers Part 3*, and *The Bottom of the Sea is Dark Part 9*.

BP: This movie opens with the twin sister of one main character's girlfriend walking near the zoo at night, alone. You guys filmed this guerrilla style, where you didn't have any permits, and you just had to show up and shoot. But the scene very specifically calls for no cars on the road, no headlights, because that would ruin the storyline. How hard was that to shoot on a road that is normally very busy with the traffic? How many takes did it require?

JO'M: We initially started filming that scene around 9:30 p.m. At 9:33 p.m., we had to end the scene, as a motorcycle passed through. We reset the shot, cleared the road once more, and began to shoot again, but a bicyclist pedaled by. We had to stop once more. After our forty-ninth take, we found ourselves looking at the bewitching hour of 3:00 a.m., and we knew this would be close to our last attempt before dawn came. If we didn't get it this time, we would just do one more after this, and that would be it. We began to film, and, would you believe it, an ice cream truck drove by. *At three in the morning. An ice cream truck.* Well, after we took a break for ice cream, we had time for one more try before sunrise. We finally got the perfect shot at 4:16 a.m., without interruption yet full of dairy. And it was beautiful—exquisite even.

BP: You only had one camera to film the whole movie, but that scene is so intense because it cuts quickly between the Howler's perspective and the fear in Brenda's eyes, then back to the Howler's perspective and again to Brenda's. And then she has to slug the Howler with her pocketbook. How difficult was it, with only one camera, to cut back-and-forth, back-and-forth, to show such intensity and suspense right out of the gate in that opening scene?

JO'M: A scene of that caliber must be filmed by an absolute genius. To express my genius, I had the vision. I had the goal in mind—simply to create a shot that would, dare I say, revolutionize filmmaking as a whole. When I handed the camera to my assistant, Willy Reed, I made him run several blocks away to get an establishing shot and jog back to our shooting location. Then he was instructed to get each shot, growing closer and closer each time to the Howler and to Brenda. It was exhausting for me to watch him go back-and-forth so many times, but, after our nineteenth trip to the shooting zone, we have what you would consider *perfection*, as you see on the screen.

BP: Critics and movie buffs frequently compare the *Howlers'* director, Wally Sampson, to Stanley Kubrick regarding perfectionism. At any point in the opening scene did you think the director was being ridiculous and should let you do your job? And, if so, what shot was that?

JO'M: I would like to avoid any comments about the director at this time. I hope you can understand.

BP: Why did you deviate from the script for certain angles without the director's approval?

JO'M: A director of photography, or anybody worth their salt in the industry, knows you must take liberties. I established an entire cinematography masterpiece with just three primary angles. Tell me if there is any director of photography or any filmmaking piece that holds to those standards? This was a challenge I was ready to accept. More of a challenge than *Dark Place Under the Ocean Part 9*—or whatever it was called.

BP: Let's compare that film to the *Howlers* movie.

JO'M: With *Howlers*, it is mostly urban based. We're looking at an urban, suburban environment, lots of concrete, trees, fencelike structures. With filming in the deep sea, a lot of water and aquatic features set them apart. Clearly there's a difference.

BP: Would you say *Howlers* ranks up there with the movies you're the proudest of and where your talent shone through?

JO'M: *Howlers* is but a blip in my many, many films historically. Just look up my list of films. Matter of fact, one moment. I'll pull it up on my phone. See? I filmed 391 movies, 276 television episodes, and three videogames. Ask me how I did that?

BP: How'd you do that?

JO'M: You're asking how somebody filmed 391 movies, 276 television shows, and multiple videogames? You want to know how? By being the best.

BP: Well, I also heard you weren't the director's first, second, or even third choice.

JO'M: Regardless of who passed over whom, I got the job, and they wanted the best.

BP: One more question—and I don't want to spoil anything that happens later in the movie or in this book—but there is a scene where a Howler rips off a character's limb. Tell me about the fistfight between you and the special effects supervisor, Greg Burgenstein, because he made the hand and the blood look so unrealistic that you couldn't work with that scene at all and how you almost walked off the set.

JO'M: With *Howlers* being the film that it is, I can't say I wanted something in the vein of Sam Raimi, who is known for excessive amounts—buckets, if you will—of gore. Just a fire hydrant unloaded, full of gore and viscera. If anybody has ever severed an arm—which I may or may not have—to see that level of blood spurting is memorable, but Burgenstein wanted a quick splash of ketchup onto the camera lens instead. We were at each other's throats. Had Burgenstein got his way, it would have been comical, and everyone would have laughed. What I created was perfection. And to circle back to your comment about Kubrick, he was an elementary pedestrian filmmaker. His cinematography holds no candle to what I created during my thirty-one years of filmmaking. I retired because nothing entertained me anymore. The industry has changed, and I want no part of it.

CHAPTER 2

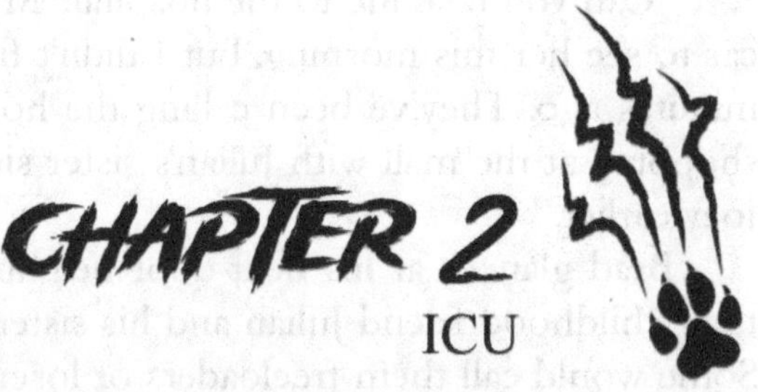

ICU

Brad rests his feet comfortably on the ottoman in front of his favorite chair, a cold Jolt Cola in one hand and the TV remote in the other. He presses the chunky Up button to flip through the thirty-six channels that his new cable box provides.

When he spots the plug-it-up opening scene to *Carrie*, he puts the remote on the arm of his couch and takes a long swig of the tonic that boasts *all the sugar and twice the caffeine*. The bubbles tickle the back of his throat, and he chokes, not on the soda goodness but because of the quick and urgent rapping on his front door.

"Coming!" he yells and swings his feet off the footrest and traipses to the door, Jolt in hand. He swings open the door to reveal a crying and shaking Barbara.

"Oh, Brad…" She collapses into his arms.

He catches her, proud of himself for not spilling any of the cola on the floor. "What's going on?" he asks, her blond ponytail tickling his nose.

Barbara pulls back and steels herself, wiping her nose with her sleeve. "Brenda has been in the ICU since last night."

Brad's heart leaps up his throat as he sets the bottle on the small table next to the door where he keeps his car keys and wallet.

"Can you take me to the hospital? My parents took the car to see her this morning, but I didn't find out until a few minutes ago. They've been calling the house, but I've been shopping at the mall with Julian's sister since I saw you and Joey earlier."

Brad glances at his next-door neighbor's house, where their childhood friend Julian and his sister still live at home. Some would call them freeloaders or losers, but Brad envies Julian with how his friend has mooched off his parents for so long.

"They must have called around because, when we got back to her house, there was a message from them to come to the hospital ASAP. So, I ran over here."

Brad scrunches his face and purses his lips. "They didn't call here to try to find you?"

"Seriously? *That* is what's gonna bother you about this situation?" Barbara places both hands on her hips and taps her foot like a rabbit, then bursts into tears.

Brad sucks her into another hug and lovingly places a hand atop her head. "C'mon. I'll take you right now."

Brad puts his arm around Barbara's shoulder as she takes a deep breath and pushes open the door to hospital room 121. Brad immediately hears the *beep-beep-beep*ing of the heart monitor, and the twin sisters' parents look up.

Their mother rises from the chair and collides with Barbara, tears staining her cheeks from hours of crying.

"Will she be okay?" Barbara pulls free from her mom's clutches and spies her sister lying on the bed, tubes and wires coming from every which way.

The twins' father, seated at the foot of the bed, pats the blanket covering Brenda's leg. "We hope so, but the doctors don't know what happened to her."

Their mom takes Barbara's hands into her own. "She lost a lot of blood."

"I think you need a break," their dad suggests to their mom. "Let's go see if anything edible is in the vending machine downstairs."

The twins' parents shamble from the room and close the door behind them, leaving Brad and Barbara with an unconscious Brenda.

Barbara sits on the bed next to her sister's chest and rests a hand on Brenda's forehead. "What happened to you?" she whispers, then lets her forehead fall onto the blanket covering Brenda's stomach. After a beat, Barbara whips her head around to face Brad. "Do you think the Talbotsville Killer did this? Or was it random?"

Brad squints to focus on the bandage around Brenda's neck. "Was she… bitten?"

Barbara grazes the bandage with her fingertips. "What kind of man would bite their victim?"

"A vampire?" Brad answers, realizing he may have inappropriately timed his attempt at comedic relief.

"Some kind of monster, for sure," Barbara mutters, then releases an extended sigh. "Can you take me home? I can't bear to see her like this. I'll go crazy and won't be good for anyone, especially my parents."

"Sure," Brad replies, his voice cracking.

Barbara interlaces her fingers with Brad's as they head for the exit, another round of sobs racking her body.

Brad pulls her close to kiss the side of her head as they turn the corner and head for the elevator. Just as the elevator doors close, he could have sworn he heard what sounded like a wolf howl far in the distance.

Hector L. Xu

Brian Paone: The hospital scene really makes the movie take a turn, so that shot was crucial. No hospital within five hundred miles would permit you to use an empty room to shoot this single yet vital scene. How did you overcome that obstacle? Especially when the director was unreachable while you scouted locations and had told you that this was a quote, unquote "you problem" and to only call him when you figured out how to fix that.

Hector L. Xu: Our location scout, Gilbert Wrensnest, tried Hope Memorial. He tried Union Station Medical. He went to every hospital within, as you said, hundreds of miles. And, for whatever reason, Gilbert got shot down. And I don't know if it was his ineptitude or if he just didn't know how to pitch what we were doing.

BP: Is it true that he even contacted a hospital in Vietnam and offered tons money to let you film there? And they gave him the Vietnamese version of a middle finger?

HLX: As I said, nobody wanted to do this. What's interesting is—I don't know how much *Howlers* trivia you know— but this was one of the last scenes we filmed, yet it's early in the film, so we were panicking. We were down to the wire. It got a little crazy. By the time we needed to film this scene, Director Sampson tasked me and three other people with a quick run to the hardware store. We picked up, I think, $320 worth of plywood, screws, two-by-fours, and we remodeled one of the crew's home bedroom. His name eludes me, but his wife was not all too thrilled. I think he was the sound guy. He could have been. Honestly I don't know, but I'm pretty sure it was the sound guy.

BP: The sound engineer's name was Willis Winston, if that rings a bell. And the assistant sound engineer was an Emily Davenport.

HLX: It's been thirty-odd years. I don't know.

BP: Thirty-nine to be exact.

HLX: It's hard to say, at this point, whose house it was. I just know we went in there at about two in the afternoon, performed a lot of demolition, replaced a lot of walls, and pulled out all the closets. We repurposed a lot of things to make it resemble a hospital room. After forty-eight hours and a second run to the hardware store for a total of $350 worth of material, we had it done. If we're looking at the current cost of that, after inflation, we're pushing thousands in just material today. We patted ourselves on the back because, looking back at it, it is still one of the best damn sets ever.

BP: That scene is so riveting because of the realism of the hospital room. You really found a way to get all the heart monitors and the hospital gurney in there. And how did you commandeer that equipment for the set? Because you can't just have a regular bed and say this is a hospital room. And, for years, nobody knew that scene wasn't in a real hospital because of the authenticity of that room.

HLX: It's funny you should mention the set dressings. Fun little fact: This is before the days of online shopping, where I'm sure you can order a hospital bed. We had a connection, which we utilized to get into one of the hospitals. I won't say which connection or which hospital. During the night hours, they wheeled out a few pieces of equipment. We took it upon ourselves to put them into the set. We shot the scene in a few short hours and returned the items to the hospital, unbeknownst to them. So, what you see in that scene, most of that is authentic equipment.

BP: In the 1998 unauthorized *Making of Howlers: The Unofficial Visual Dictionary* coffee table book, it states the bed you took from the hospital had a dying elderly woman in it, and you gently laid her on the floor and then put her back in bed when you returned the bed after the scene was shot.

HLX: I didn't lay anyone on the floor. What I did was tell them where to place the bed within the set for the best lighting and for the best angles. The person who pulled the person from the bed? That's between them, the hospital, and that lovely woman who loaned us her bed.

CHAPTER 3
BECOMING THE BEAST

Hospital room 121 is dark and vacant, except for the patient lying on the bed. Her parents went home when visiting hours ended. Silence fills the room, save the constant and steady beeping of the heart monitor. Moonlight shines through the window, slowly reaching upward with each passing hour.

A gasp infiltrates the stillness and the beeping, which gives way to labored breathing. The sound of air sucking through mucus, then exhaling through fluid, overpowers the heart monitor's sounds. The gasp from under the blanket graduates to a fluttering groan, not unlike a loud snore. Or a death rattle.

The shape under the blanket tenses all its muscles, and its hands grip the sides of the bed. Its back arches. The heart monitor's beeping increases in tempo.

Brenda shoves a fistful of blanket into her mouth to stifle her scream and to bite on something that may alleviate the cracking of bones happening to her skeleton underneath her skin and muscles. Sweat beads on her forehead, then streaks her face, commingling with tears draining from her eyes.

Brenda flails onto her right side, then her left, so violently that the bed shifts a few inches across the floor, and the bandage around her neck comes free. She grabs the raised corner and rips it from her skin, wailing and writhing. Her fingers and other bones continue to shatter, reforming at different lengths and thicknesses, while she grips the octopus-like plethora of wires and tubes attached to her and then forcefully yanks.

The heart monitor machine silences, leaving the sounds of bones snapping and the machinegun-like grunting coming from the hospital bed.

Brenda catches her breath for just a moment, long enough to fling the blanket off her, and beelines for the bathroom. As she is about to cross the threshold, a tsunami of spasms rack her body from within every one of her molecules and launches her into the corner before she can enter the bathroom.

She claws at her face, her nails digging into newly wrinkled skin, her fingertips pricked by coarse hairs springing from her cheeks and forehead. She screams as she feels pointy ears grow from the crown of her head. She grimaces as her teeth elongate, and then her nose and mouth extend, morphing into a snout.

And the pain and torment end just as abruptly as it started… replaced only with the same intensity of another feeling.

A desire to feed…

Brenda-Wolf snorts and growls low in her throat as she lowers one fur-covered shoulder and sprints for the closed window. She feels instant rejuvenation as she steps into the pathway of the moonlight coming through the windowpanes. She does not even notice when her body breaks the glass nor when she falls two stories and lands on the asphalt parking lot.

Brenda-Wolf belts out the first of many howls as she scampers and disappears into the woods behind the hospital.

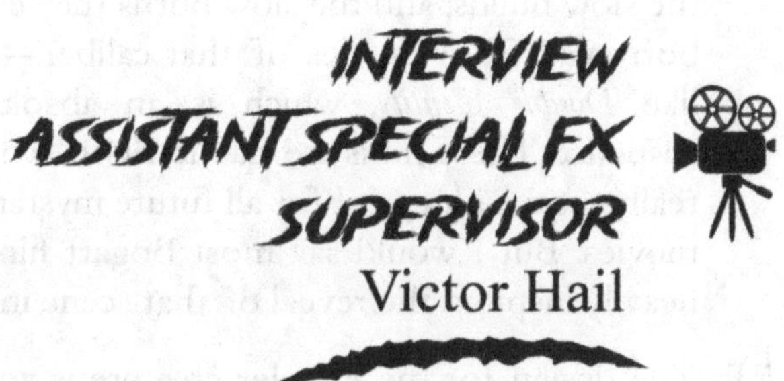

Victor Hail

Brian Paone: The third major scene of the film is when Brenda transforms from a human into a Howler, in the makeshift hospital room that we discussed previously with the set designer. When Brenda goes into the corner outside the bathroom, nobody who sees the movie for the first time expects her to turn around as a Howler. We think maybe she contracted an infection, and she might die. So when Brenda turns around and is now a full-blooded Howler and so meticulously detailed, it terrifies people even to this day, even after they've seen the scene dozens of times. No one is ever ready for that moment. What other classic films inspired those effects?

Victor Hail: When you draw from other films, you don't want to draw from obvious ones within your genre. We looked for films that had reveals which astonished the viewer, that made the viewer gasp or other reactions you would realistically have. The biggest title we would throw around was *The Maltese Falcon*. When studying suspenseful movies like that one, or even Hitchcock's hit *Rope*—which, as we know today, is one of the most popular Hitchcock films to grace the silver screen—each of these films have a level of suspense yet to be mirrored. We essentially wore out the Betamax, rewatching and rewatching, just to study the pull-aways, the slow builds, and the slow burns they established. We borrowed from movies of that caliber—even a movie like *Double Identity*, which is an absolute classic in suspense. These films are classic 1940s' works of art that really set the blueprint for all future mystery or suspense movies. But I would say most Bogart films of that era heavily inspired the reveal of that scene in *Howlers*.

BP: The design for the Howler creature is something we'd never seen in film before. It's so unique and inspiring. I realize you're just the assistant, and your job was to assist the supervisor, but did you have any input on the final Howler design or how the makeup artist, Sankeet Kapur, applied the special effects costume onto the actor?

VH: To say I just assisted is an understatement, considering our lead actress was usually buried face-first in a plate of snow, if you catch my drift. But it was the eighties. That's what people did. This, the creation of the Howler that we know and see, is actually the eleventh iteration. However, I could be mistaken, so if you need to verify this information with someone else, please do. And, if you'll need to update this interview, by all means, just correct my answer.

BP: Maybe for the forty-ninth anniversary.

VH: If only we had kept the napkin that we drew the original Howler design on… We were at a diner, hanging out. I believe after three milkshakes, the original Howler was conceived. And it is a far cry from what you see today on the screen.

BP: I'm sure that napkin would go for a pretty penny at an auction, if someone still had it.

VH: We threw away that napkin with the rest of the rubbish.

BP: How long did Jennipher Johns, the lead actress who plays Brenda and Barbara, sit in the chair to apply all that realistic latex, before shooting her Howler scenes?

VH: I don't know if you're familiar with some of the lore of the making of this film, but we shot that hospital scene, where Brenda is revealed as a Howler, over the span of four days. The first time we applied the prosthetics was a fourteen-hour process. By the fourth day of shooting that scene, we had it down to about six hours, which is impressive if you have to sit almost motionless in a makeup chair for even that long. Anybody who has done that knows we don't have Game Boys or whatever people have today to entertain them. I believe they would play on their cellphones nowadays. Back then, you would just stare into the mirror.

BP: During a now-famous and teary-eyed *Oprah Winfrey Show* episode from 1996, Jennipher Johns publicly acknowledged her claustrophobia and agoraphobia, then revealed how that had led to outbursts and panic attacks during the latex-application process. She stated that she would ask you to get her out of the costume, but you were already ten, maybe eleven, hours in. How did you deal with Jennipher Johns's anxiety underneath all that restricting makeup?

VH: We applied the makeup multiple times over many days of shooting. In one instance, we had just finished the application. I don't remember who was bringing the material, but we were pasting on the last few tufts of hair to flush out some of the latex on the side of her face. Out of nowhere, Jennipher began to just claw at her own face and removed all the makeup. Now this is the

1980s. What is the street-level equivalent? Spirit gum, if you will. But we weren't using spirit gum. We used a high-end adhesive, designed for long-term makeup applications that survived under sweat and intense heat and lighting. It did end up scarring her face slightly. I heard through the rumor mill that she definitely was a little upset about these things.

BP: She was also simultaneously filming another movie—the one that got her nominated for an Academy Award—and they had to rewrite the script to explain how her character in that movie got scars on her face, all because of the Howler makeup. Do you ever think to yourself, maybe the director casted the wrong actress for that part?

VH: I believed in the director's vision. Mr. Sampson had made up his mind. You know, if you talk to George Lucas, Harrison Ford was it. He *was* Han Solo. That was exactly how this film was made.

BP: So you think Director Sampson saw Jennipher Johns and said, "That's my lead Howler?"

VH: I would like to say yes. I think that would be a factual statement.

BP: Discuss the allegations of the unethical ways you obtained the hair for the Howler prosthetics.

VH: I'm going to interrupt you right there. Yes, these family pets were shaved, but we had written permission from the owners. We did our best to only get huskies and other shaggy dogs that had the right length and consistency for the Howler hair. So, before you even go down this road, I've spoken with PETA. I've spoken with everybody. I can't tell you the number of press conferences I've had to do. I was on an interweb's cast of pod—whatever they are called—where we discussed the same thing. I'm not palavering about this anymore. We had the pet owner's permission. Thank you.

CHAPTER 4
JOEY GETS THE SCOOP

Joey skips up Brad's front steps to the porch and rings his brother's doorbell. Rustling and sounds of fiddling with the locks morph into the knob turning and the door swinging open. Joey smiles at his brother, then his expression immediately falls into a frown and furrowed brows as he hears Barbara sobbing from somewhere within the house.

Brad steps aside. "You should hear what happened. Come in."

Joey nervously fingers the Nikon camera resting against his stomach, hung from a strap around his neck, as he walks through the house toward the rear.

Barbara wipes tear-stained eyes with the back of her hand and clears her throat. "She's *gone!*"

Joey quizzically side-eyes his brother.

"Have a seat. Can I get you a Jolt?" Brad asks.

Joey shakes his head; every second that they are not explaining what is wrong, besides Barbara's sister being in the ICU, stretches into what feels like an hour.

Brad snatches a bag of Reese Pieces from the end table and plops onto the orange couch. "Brenda went missing in the middle of the night."

Joey stands ramrod straight, all his senses on high alert. "What?… What do you mean, went *missing?*"

"The nurses heard a crash from her hospital room, and, when they went to check on her, she was gone, and the window was shattered," Brad adds. "As if she had jumped through it."

"Did they find her…" Joey gulps. "Her body?" He winces when the last word escapes his mouth.

Barbara shakes her head and runs across the room to bury herself in Brad's chest.

Brad pats her back and regards his little brother. "The whole town is out looking for her, but the police have no leads. And she's not the first one to disappear since you've been away at college."

Joey's eyes alight with realization. *This could be the article I've been waiting for. A woman escaped from the hospital? I gotta get the scoop on this!*

Joey navigates the sleepy streets of Talbotsville on foot, his handy-dandy notepad at the ready and his lucky pen tapping his mouth in deep thought. His trusty black Nikon camera hangs around his neck, landing at stomach level, as he adjusts his black thick-rimmed glasses.

Joey scans his handwritten list of the people who have gone missing since the start of the year—all attributed to the Talbotsville Killer. However, with Brenda vanishing from the hospital, Joey contemplates that maybe something else is afoot—something more sinister. Nefarious even.

The young wannabe reporter checks the numbers on the mailbox and matches them with the first line in his notepad, *47 West Broadway.* This is the house. Joey musters his most nonthreatening and nonintrusive smile and rings the bell.

The door opens, exposing an older lady with her hair in rollers, wearing a pink nightgown and bunny slippers. "Can I help you, young man?"

Joey adjusts his glasses and squints from the sun reflecting off the second-story windows. "I hate to bother you, ma'am, but I was wondering if you could tell me a little about your granddaughter, who has been missing."

Joey steels his breath, waiting for her rejection, followed by a door slammed in his face.

Instead the woman softens her glare. "Are you a reporter?"

Joey flashes his puppy-dog smile as a burst of warmth and confidence cycles through his body. "Why, yes, ma'am. That is certainly what I am."

The woman turns and disappears into the foyer. "Come in. Do you like tea?"

Joey declines the tea, yet follows her to a living room, where he sits on the blue couch, his back ramrod straight to appear more professional, more crucial.

The woman returns from the kitchen with a steaming teacup, a string with the tea company's logo on a square tag hanging over the rim. She sits delicately across from him in what looks like a brand-new recliner. "My granddaughter left her boyfriend Charlie's house after dinner one night in April to go to work and never came back." She takes her first careful and deliberate sip of tea.

Joey scribbles the words *Charlie* and *April* into his notepad, then sticks the end of the pen into his mouth to contemplate his next question. "Could you describe your granddaughter and what she was wearing that night? And do you think Charlie had anything to do with it?"

"Oh, goodness gracious no. Charlie hasn't slept a wink in weeks, heading the search party for her. She was wearing some band tee-shirt that she also has a poster of in her room."

"Do you know the name of the band?" Joey scribes more notes.

"I don't, but the poster in her room has the words *Hungry Like the Wolf* under their faces." She shrugs.

Joey writes *Duran Duran tee-shirt* on his notepad, then combs his unruly hair with his fingers. "And where does she work?"

"At the animal shelter, but at night. In charge of feeding the animals and cleaning their cages. She never arrived."

"So, what I'm hearing is that she disappeared somewhere between Charlie's house and the pound." Joey thinks he is better at this reporting business than he thought. He silently pats himself on the back for getting so much pertinent information so quickly from a stranger. Maybe this *is* the right career path for him after all. Maybe… a Pulitzer is in his future.

"That's right. Never made it to work." The woman adjusts her nightgown where it drapes over her knees. "I hope that helps, but that's all the information I have."

Joey springs to his feet with zeal. "Oh, this is great information, ma'am. After talking to you, I feel I am one step closer to cracking this case."

"Glad I could help." The woman rises to escort Joey from the house. "Please let me know if you find out anything else about my sweet granddaughter."

"Oh, I certainly will." Joey smiles and untangles the strap from his camera that spun when he stood.

Once outside in the Talbotsville sunlight, Joey feels a new sense of vigor, confident he will write the article to blow open this whole story and to expose the truth.

He hopes the editor at his college newspaper will be proud.

Joey raps his knuckles on the door of 333 Wonderview Avenue and waits, surveying the street behind him and noticing how eerily quiet the town seems on this Saturday morning.

The door opens to expose an overweight and balding man, his white undershirt sullied with yellow and brown stains, and forget about a five-o'clock shadow. Joey thinks the man's scruff represents more of a 3:00 a.m. shadow after a night of hard drinking. The man blows a puff of cigar smoke into Joey's face, then lowers his hand by his leg, letting the cigar smoke tendrils rise to partially block his face.

"Can I help ya, boy?"

Joey coughs and waves away the smoke in front of his face. "I was wondering if I could talk to you about your sister, who I heard—"

The door slams shut, leaving Joey alone on the stoop, and the deadbolt turns and clicks into its locked position. He sighs and recites an internal motivational soliloquy to lift his spirits from the gross old man's rejection.

Joey crosses off the man's address from his notepad and trots down the front steps to head toward house number three from the list.

When he reaches 242 Lestor Lowe Row, he whistles and raises an eyebrow at the fleet of vehicles in the driveway: a brand-new red Camaro IROC-Z with a T-roof, a burgundy Pontiac Firebird Trans Am, and a slick black Chevrolet Monte Carlo. Joey cranes his neck to see farther into the driveway, where his childhood obsession with vintage vehicles comes in handy to identify the Rolls Royce Phantom sitting inside an open double-car garage, nestled snuggly next to a pristine stainless-steel DeLorean.

"Hoity-toity," he mutters as he approaches the sprawling three-story mansion's front door.

He presses the illuminated doorbell and listens to the singsong of chimes from inside the residence. They ring for what feels like an unnecessary amount of time, until Joey cocks his head and realizes these people's doorbell plays *Fur Elise* in its entirety.

"Hoity-toity for sure," he mocks and chortles to himself.

The door opens, and Joey's breath hitches in his lungs.

The young woman's golden locks blow perfectly upward, as if a fan were positioned right at her head from on the floor.

Time stops. Sunlight breaks through the clouds. The hand of God descends from the heavens and lands on Joey's shoulders. He hears a choir of cherubs singing in the background behind him. Her teeth sparkle when she smiles.

She asks, "Umm… may I help you?"

Her voice breaks Joey's illusion, and he stares at his shoes, embarrassed that she caught him ogling her. No, not ogling. More like worshiping, as she appears to be an angel incarnate.

"My… my name is Joey. I'm… I'm a reporter and wanted to… um… talk about your brother?"

The angel purses her lips and peers over Joey's shoulder. Just when he thinks her reaction conveys anger, and she might dismiss him with a door slam, she refocuses on his eyes and softens her expression.

"The police swore us to secrecy. How do you know about him?"

Joey furrows his brows in confusion but realizes that a good reporter—and that is what he is turning into this morning, goshdarnit—keeps a poker face and reminds himself that he is the one to ask the questions.

Joey shifts his weight onto his toes and rolls back onto his heels. "Well, that's how good I am." He raises his Nikon camera to chin level. "See? Even have the gear and everything."

The young woman giggles and covers her mouth, as if letting sounds of joy escape her might somehow diminish the gravity of the situation. "Come in. I'm housesitting for my parents."

"Oh? My parents are gone for the week too," Joey exclaims, then scrunches his face, balls his fists, and curses himself for sounding like an excited and horny high-schooler, trying to invite the prom queen to an unchaperoned house party.

"You're funny." She giggles again. "And kinda cute."

Joey and his reddened face follow her through the sprawling foyer, with a chandelier adorning the ceiling, and into a sitting room.

The young woman takes a framed photo off the mantel and hands it to Joey. "This is him. The police found his body mutilated at Landis Lake last week." She meets Joey's gaze. "They insisted that they would not release this information to the public, to keep panic at a minimum."

Joey returns the picture to her. "The town is already going crazy with the disappearances. I can see how adding mutilation to the equation could create bedlam."

She snorts. "Bedlam? You're adorable."

Joey kicks one shoe with the other and sighs out a "Shucks."

"So, are you any closer to finding the killer? Because it looks like the cops don't have any leads. They also told us that my brother was not the only maimed body they have found at the lake."

Joey's gaze pierces hers. "What? You mean the police have been covering up multiple mutilated bodies?"

She nods. "Are you gonna print this in your article? I think the town should know. It might save more lives."

Joey adjusts his glasses, then taps his pen against his notepad. "You betch'ya! My brother's girlfriend's twin sister went missing from the hospital after an attack outside the zoo. I think it's time I pay a visit to Landis Lake."

"Be careful." She delicately grabs his forearm. "And I hope you get the scoop you need to blow this story wide open."

"I do too. And thank you for the information."

She grins at him and heads for the front door. When she opens it, Joey goes to step outside but stops in the doorway and faces her.

"Maybe when this is over, and, if I don't die, would you like to get some milkshakes and maybe see a movie?"

She sucks her lips into her mouth and smirks. "I would love that, reporter boy. I've been dying to see *Ferris Bueller's Day Off*." She winks at him.

Joey swallows hard and adjusts the invisible collar of an imaginary button-up shirt that he isn't wearing to get more air into his lungs. "Well, let me crack this case and get the scoop so I can save the town and get the girl!"

She waves goodbye to him by waggling her fingers up and down, then closes the door.

Joey circles her address in his notepad and bounds with a newfound bounce toward Landis Lake. Then he slaps his forehead with the realization that he never got her name.

Brian Paone: Nell San Pablo, thank you for speaking with me. You were the boom operator for what's considered one of the most cult classic films of the last millennia. Do you realize that?

Nell San Pablo: Is it?

BP: According to all the screenings that still happen all over the country, it is.

NSP: Well, that's news to me. I don't know what to tell you.

BP: Do you remember the scene, Joey Gets the Scoop? This is when Joey interviews three different people whose loved ones disappeared during the Howler invasion.

NSP: I suppose. Wait. What scene are you talking about?

BP: The one when Joey goes to a grandmother's house whose granddaughter has turned into a Howler, dubbed lovingly throughout the years by the fans as the Duran Duran Howler. Do you remember how difficult it was to hold the boom mic for that dialogue exchange?

NSP: You're talking about the woman who was in the wheelchair? The woman who we had to relocate from a wheelchair to a recliner because she kept rolling around, and we kept hearing crushing garbage?

BP: Wrong movie.

NSP: No? It had to be the one at the nursing home.

BP: Different movie.

NSP: Was it the one at the grocery store?

BP: Again, different movie.

NSP: Well then, I don't know.

BP: I'll jog your memory on another scene. The second person Joey interviews is a cantankerous older man, wearing a stained undershirt, and doesn't want to talk to Joey, so he slams the door in Joey's face. Do you remember how hard it was to move the boom mic quick enough from the entryway so it would not be in the camera shot when the man slams the door in Joey's face?

NSP: This scene doesn't ring any bells, but you're telling me that I had a boom in a door, and—what did you say?— the door slammed on the mic? That doesn't sound like something I would do. Sounds like you didn't do your research.

BP: The third character may jog your memory because she became the wet dream of every teenage boy in the theater. Joey refers to her as the Blonde Goddess. She opens the door, and the director of photography had an angle where the sunlight descends on Joey's head to show how striking this young woman is to him. In the 1997 special-edition DVD remaster, Director Sampson digitally added a twinkle to one of her teeth, which caused a whole bunch of problems with the purists of the *Howler* universe. You must remember how this woman fawns over Joey, and he ogles her, and they make a date to see *Ferris Bueller's Day Off*, if they both survive the Howler invasion.

NSP: Doesn't sound familiar.

BP: You don't remember the Blonde Goddess? She's been in calendars, posters on teenage boys' walls. She's considered the Pamela Anderson of *Baywatch* for *Howlers*. You mean to tell me that doesn't ring a bell at all?

NSP: Do you happen to have a photo or anything?

BP: Have you even seen the movie since it came out?

NSP: No, I don't care to watch anything I've ever done. I worked on two films as the boom operator. They paid me fifty bucks, and I was gone. I don't even know why you're here. Do you have a photo of this woman or not?

BP: You can look her up on your phone. Just type in *Howler Blonde Goddess*.

NSP: Are you talking about one of them smart cellular devices?

BP: Okay, let's change gears and just discuss equipment, since you can't remember *Howlers* specifically. What brand of boom mic do you prefer to use in your movies?

NSP: Whatever they hand me for the fifty bucks. I stood there and held a stick. I don't know what you're getting at, boy.

BP: All right, I appreciate your time.

NSP: Why don't you appreciate your time somewhere else? Maybe you can take it out of this house. Go on now, you get.

CHAPTER 5
WHO'S HUNTING WHO?

Thinking that Landis Lake may hold some answers, Joey strides toward the outskirts of town, his camera bouncing against his stomach with each step. He also realizes he might find Brenda in the lake area too—hopefully still alive and not in a mauled state.

The walk from suburbia to the wooded and more secluded area of Talbotsville may have taken most of the afternoon, but, to Joey, it only takes a few moments, as he spends the time lost in his thoughts—thoughts that include a serial killer, citizens disappearing, other citizens found dismembered, and of a blonde angel who lives on Lestor Lowe Row.

The sun started its descent behind the lake, giving wide berth for the moon to begin its night shift, until the celestial bodies switch roles again at dawn. Joey enters the dirt path that bisects the woods, leading to the lake.

Joey's sneakers crunch below him, and he hears rustling keeping pace with him from the woods. He bites the inside of his cheek to keep his anxiety at bay and to keep his feet moving forward toward the lake—not retreating to the safety of the town.

Joey spots a rustling bush from his peripheral vision and quickens his stride. He grips his camera to prevent it from banging against his stomach, with his accelerated gait.

The rustling grows louder and more pronounced. Yep, Joey is sure now that something is matching his speed alongside him within the shadows of the trees.

He halts when he thinks he hears a snort. Or a growl?

His heart beats loudly in his ears, drowning out the sounds he is trying to hear. The movement seems to have stopped when he stopped. Is someone—or some*thing*—following him?

Or worse, he thinks… *tracking* him?

He gulps down the saliva collected in his mouth and powers forward.

The rustling starts again with Joey's steps. Without slowing this time, he holds his breath, conjuring as much courage as he can, and sneaks a glance to where the sound is coming from.

Joey's eyes widen when he spots what appears to be two tall and furry ears moving at his pace. He quickly focuses on the dirt path in front of him, his heart hammering in his chest. Then he has an idea. The problem is that this idea may either solidify him as possibly the greatest reporter who ever lived or will bring his swift demise, adding him to the list of missing locals. Or worse, adding him to the secret list of mutilated victims.

But no award-winning reporter made a name for themselves by playing it safe, he reminds himself. So Joey raises his camera without looking at his target, keeping his gaze on the pathway to the lake, not slowing his trajectory, and lets his index finger snap the shutter button like a pneumonic drill.

Chck! Chck! Chck! Chck! goes the camera, the sound amplifies in the hush of the woods.

Everything happens so fast, yet feels so slow, that Joey reacts purely on reflex and not on any masterplan. Just as the dirt path expands to reveal Landis Lake, the rising moonlight glittering off the water's calm surface, the furry-eared creature bursts from the wood line toward Joey.

But Joey again mashes the shutter button as he breaks into a sprint for the lake. The creature howls a sound that sends shivers down Joey's spine, and he finds better purchase on the ground to help propel him faster toward the open lake. However, he is still undecided on what he plans to do when he gets to the water.

Maybe the creature can't swim, he muses.

Joey figures he has snapped enough photos of the killer now to give the police a solid lead, as well as for his own article for the college newspaper, and snuggles the camera to his chest to become a bit stealthier.

The creature howls again and shortens the distance between them, two of Joey's strides equaling only one of the creature's. Joey steals a peek behind him at a furry paw reaching for his shirt, its claws just a few inches from grabbing their prize.

Joey screams so loud that his voice cracks, then just air comes from his throat. He realizes he could either fight or continue to flee.

Always considering himself to be a lover and not a fighter—and realizing that has gotten him nowhere in life, and nowhere fast—Joey grinds his heels into the dirt and spins about.

Face-to-face with the wolflike creature, Joey ducks his head and removes his camera in one swift stroke. The surprise of the creature's knife-long teeth and its Duran Duran tee-shirt makes Joey pause just long enough for the furry paw to collide with the side of his head. A burst of pain follows, and red dots bloom in his vision. Joey grabs the side of his injured face and feels the gooey stickiness of what must be his blood.

The creature sticks out its chest, pulls its arms behind itself, and howls at the moon in assured triumph.

Flashing through his mind are images of desecrated bodies, a missing Brenda, and a blonde goddess sitting next to him in a movie theater—after he has saved the town. Those help summon Joey's courage and strength to take a swing, camera in hand for added force, at the creature's snout.

Joey's fist finds its mark, and the wolf-thing stumbles backward, with startle and surprise flashing in its still-human eyes, until its tattered sneaker clips a protruding rock and sends the creature flailing backward into some shrubbery.

Joey understands that his bravado just bought him a few precious seconds to escape and that he could not acquire this gift so easily a second time, so he digs his heels into the pathway and sprints like a gazelle.

When Joey knows he is all out of gas—his lungs burning and heaving—he slows and enters the openness between the woods and the shoreline of Landis Lake. He spots a bench one dozen yards away and stumbles toward it. Once seated, he inspects his camera for damage. When he doesn't find a cracked lens or any missing pieces, his eyes widen at the sight of the clump of blood and fur stuck to the side of the camera, right where he landed the blow to the wolf creature.

Joey glances at the moon high above the lake and smiles. He knows exactly what to do with this evidence. And it may just give them all the answers to uncover this godforsaken mystery.

Brian Paone: Today I'm speaking with the owner of Wonderwolves Incorporated—the animal handlers for the movie. Could you introduce yourself please.

Hans: Hi, I'm actually *ze* co-owner. My name *iz* Hans. My co-owner actually passed away. Very tragic, very sad.

BP: How did your co-owner pass away?

Hans: Very tragic, very sad. It was very tragic, very sad. One of *ze* animals, *ze* wolf. *Ze* wolf *iz* a magnificent creature, and sometimes *zey're* just a wild animal. My co-owner tragically passed away from *ze* heart attack.

BP: Nothing to do with a wolf at all?

Hans: It was because of working with *ze* wolves. Heart was so big. Heart was so big. It wouldn't fit in *hiz* chest anymore.

BP: Joey wins a fight against a Howler on the pathway through the woods to Landis Lake, which shows us that someone can escape unscathed from a Howler attack. Is it true that you had dozens of real wolves on set during that scene to help the actor inside that Howler costume get into character?

Hans: *Yez, thiz* was unique because what we wanted to do was have *ze* actors, they got to observe *ze* wolves, but what was unique was, when the actor was in *ze* Howler outfit, *zey* would observe *ze* actor in *ze* Howler outfit to understand what *ze* Howler was. *Zis* was revolutionary at the time. One of *ze* most unique uses of *ze* wolves being trained by humans, but not in *ze* way that you do typically, with *ze* clicker or *ze* positive reinforcement. You simply have *zem* observe *ze* wolves that were actually people dressed as *ze* wolves. It was a unique symbiosis.

BP: When the Howler attacks Joey, did your wolves feel a kinship to the creature and want to help attack Joey, not realizing they're observing filmmaking?

Hans: So, with *ze* wolves, with *ze* wolves, several moments, we would explain to *ze* wolves that *zis iz* a film and not to be considered real.

BP: And the wolves understood that?

Hans: *Ze* wolves seemed to have understood , how you *zay*, the film versus a real life. *Zey* would watch. *Zey* would take note, and, from *zere*, we only had one incident with Felipe.

BP: Was Felipe a wolf or a handler?

Hans: Yes. He was a… Felipe was very, very smart. Felipe was very, very advanced for a person. Felipe was sleeping with wolves, not in that way, not in a dirty way, in the comfort and camaraderie way. He became too overwhelmed with excitement and attacked a stuntman in *ze* leg, biting him, but *ze* human bite *iz* not strong as *ze* wolf, but only *zree* teeth broken.

BP: Your wolves only understand German. Did they ever get confused with the English-speaking actors, or did you have German translators helping the wolves to understand the plotline?

Hans: We would often run *ze*, how you *zay*, the title underneath, the subliminal title, *zey* would run, as *ze* wolves could understand *ze* English and *ze* Deutsch words, and *zey* would make *ze* correlation. And I believe some of *ze* wolves learn English alongside *ze* native tongue, and *zey* went on to work on *ze* other films, such as *The Dance with* ze *Wolves*. I know *zey* went on to work on several films using *ze* newfound English capabilities.

BP: The *Howlers* experience for your company opened many doors and took you guys into almost superstardom of film wolf handlers.

Hans: Yeah, yeah, yeah. *Zometimes* *ze* director do not use our wolves. Leonardo DiCaprio, he was in movie about *ze* wolves, but no need our wolf. So, we were unfortunately unable to secure a role in *ze* film.

BP: One of the wolves gave birth on set while they filmed when the Howler attacks Joey. A lot of casual viewers don't realize that, offscreen, most of your staff were scrambling to safely deliver a wolf cub, while they filmed the shot we see in the film now. How chaotic was that moment for you?

Hans: Yeah, yeah, yeah. That was very exciting. That was *ze* beautiful moment. If you look at *ze* scene, when Joey—Joey was the man fighting *ze* Howler—*ze* scene when *ze* two grappled. If you look just off *ze* side, you almost *zee* the foot of *ze* pregnant wolf. It's very beautiful. But now, I believe *zey*, how you *zay*? Digitally removed?

BP: Right. The director digitally removed the paw for the 1997 special-edition DVD remaster. A lot of fans are angry that the original theatrical version is unavailable because Wally Sampson—I believe you were the only one who had a good working experience with him—wants the 1997 version to be the quintessential version because of those newly added digital touch-ups.

Hans: Yeah, so *ze* director, he would wear *ze* Howler head to speak with *ze* wolves. He would, he would often dine with *zem*. He would make, make urines on different property to assert dominance. He was, he was very immersed in role.

BP: My last question, because it's such a sweet story—you named that cub a very special name. Could you tell everyone its name?

Hans: Yeah, yeah. So it was, so you're talking about *ze* cub, yeah? The one that was born on *ze* set? We all, we all loves greatly. It was, it was adorable. Did not have a name for *ze* first two weeks. But we all settled on *Einen Kot Nehmen*, which was a beautiful name. *Ja, ja.* Ze cub passed away two years, two years today actually. And *ze* last great acting movie for *ze* cub was, it was *ze* stunt double for *ze* live action *Jungle Book*.

BP: Wasn't the cub also slated to work on the live action *Lion King*? But it fell into the circle of life? [A very long awkward moment of silence follows, while he glares at me.]

Hans: Yeah, yeah, yeah. *Ze* circle of *ze* life. It's actually very sad and tragic. It's not funny. All right, we're done here.

CHAPTER 6

NIGHT HIKE AT LANDIS LAKE

Joey's smile slowly returns to a stoic expression when he hears rustling from the pathway to his left—not the same one he used to get here while fleeing from the wolf-thing.

He secures his camera around his neck and ducks behind the bench to watch. He is sure he didn't kill the Duran Duran–fan wolf creature, maybe just knocked it out. So, if more of those things come down the other path, Joey may have to just accept that he is trapped without an escape route. He eyes the motionless water and reminds himself to swim across the lake as his last-ditch effort to safety. Fingers crossed that these furry cryptids don't know how to doggy-paddle.

Two teens, holding hands, the girl swinging a woven picnic basket in her free hand, emerge from the second pathway and enter the openness of the shoreline. Their giggles and the boy's flirtatious teasing seem amplified in the stillness of the moonlit lake, all within the ominous dangers that may remain in the looming shadows of trees.

"Psst!" Joey rises slowly from behind the bench.

The couple pays him no mind, the picnic basket swinging haphazardly and with abandon at the girl's side.

"Hey!" Joey yells but in a whisper.

The boy stops and regards the man standing behind the bench. "Get back, Luna. We can't trust anyone anymore."

Joey chuckles to himself. *Luna? That's rich.*

"You think he might be the Talbotsville Killer?" the girl chokes out.

"Can't be too cautious." The boy raises his voice to acknowledge Joey. "Just stay there, mister. You come any closer, and I'll kill you. I have a gun."

Joey recognizes the nervous waver in the boy's voice to signify that the boy is fibbing. "I am a friend." Joey slaps his forehead; isn't that what all kidnappers and child molesters say just before they ask if their unsuspecting victim wants to see a van full of free puppies? "I mean, I am a news reporter. Joey Bradshaw." He waggles his camera in the air to prove his claim.

The boy relaxes a bit. "What are you doing hiding behind the bench? At night?"

"Are you hunting the killer?" the girl asks, her eyes wide in admiration.

"Sort of. However, I think we're dealing with *killers*. Plural."

The teens exchange a horrified look, then Luna cocks her head at Joey. "What makes you think—"

Four distinct growls emerge from the trees behind Joey, exposing four wolf creatures, all different heights and sizes, wearing the same clothes they were donning whenever they were… taken and transformed.

Luna screams, drops the picnic basket—spilling cold cuts and fruit salad all over the ground—and bolts for the pathway where Joey killed or just knocked out the Duran Duran–fan wolf.

"Wait!" Joey yells, trying to stop her. "I don't know if that path is—"

The previously unconscious wolf creature appears from nowhere, as if transported from the netherworld, and, in one swift gnaw, rips Luna's windpipe from her throat, her blood sputtering like a geyser. Luna's body crumples to the pathway, and her boyfriend screams.

Joey trips and stumbles over the bench, then finds purchase when one of the horde's paws land on his collar. Joey kicks into overdrive, like the Flash himself, toward the pathway where the teens appeared from. His camera violently bounces against his stomach, and his glasses slide down his nose while he runs.

Joey hears Luna's boyfriend release a bloodcurdling scream from behind him.

… and then silence.

Killers. Plural.

Brian Paone: When we first see Landis Lake in the film, the moon is so vivid and so crisp. Did you guys wait to shoot that on a perfect full moon night? Because it is just perfection for that scene.

Gilbert Wrensnest III: When we shot on scene for the lake, every day was overcast unfortunately, and, on the only day the moon was visible, it was in a waning gibbous. Quickly thinking, I used some of our special effects design team and our director of photography. Then, with some clever camera angles, while using a Frisbee, two flashlights, and a golf ball, we simulated a full moon. Not to pat myself on the back, but it looks pretty damn good.

BP: Yes, and, as the fans know, Director Sampson is vehemently against CGI and digital effects, which is why he made everybody use practical effects for *Howlers*. However, how did you feel when Sampson released the 1997 special-edition DVD remaster? He replaced your practical effect with a moon clearly rendered in a computer via the early 1990s.

GWIII: Well, it all comes down to money. He wants to squeeze the viewers for what he can. We don't consider him a purist. He's strictly there to enhance his product, to make it, do I say, relevant to a newer generation? But looking back, at that day and age, if you watch the original cut, the special effects hold up today. That's the beauty of practical effects. Any film that has practical effects still looks beautiful. But what you got when you created a film with a processor in the 1990s was something grainy and childish-looking. That's what you're getting with the special edition.

BP: Landis Lake is considered the Holy Land, the mecca of *Howlers* fans. People have spent the last thirty-nine years trying to locate the real lake where you shot this scene. Companies even offer tours for fans to try to find the shooting location, like Landis Lake is Bigfoot or Loch Ness or something. You spent your whole career with the motto, Mum's the word. You appeared on the *Phil Donahue Show* when his ratings were declining, and you got into a fistfight backstage with his producer because you chose not to reveal the location during the show. Yet, you had agreed that his show would contain the big reveal, and he had been heavily advertising that angle for this episode. When you went live on the air, that episode broke all records for viewership for his show. And you let him down. Then later, when you were interviewed for the *Making of Howlers: The Unauthorized Visual Dictionary* coffee table book in 1998, you refused to disclose the location. I'm asking you now, for this very special thirty-ninth anniversary of the film and this novelization, could you please finally tell the fans where they can pilgrimage to the real Landis Lake?

GWIII: It is actually Wagner Valley Lake. That beautiful pristine lake was located just out back of a nice cul-de-sac, where we used one of those homes for an interior shot. That lake has since dried up, and I believe those homes were sold and demolished and turned into a Walmart. So, if you're looking for it, you won't find it anymore, unless you need to shop at Walmart.

BP: Fans usually mention *Monster Squad* when naming horror movies from the later part of the 1980s that *Howlers* inspired. Without that landscape, the fans would not revere *Howlers* the way they do. Some might say, if it weren't for the locations you chose, the film would not be half of the movie that it is. That's hard to do, shot after shot, scene after scene. Do you feel that getting the movie to look that way was just lightning in a bottle? Or was it your keen eye and talent for finding all these spots?

GWIII: I *am* lightning in a bottle.

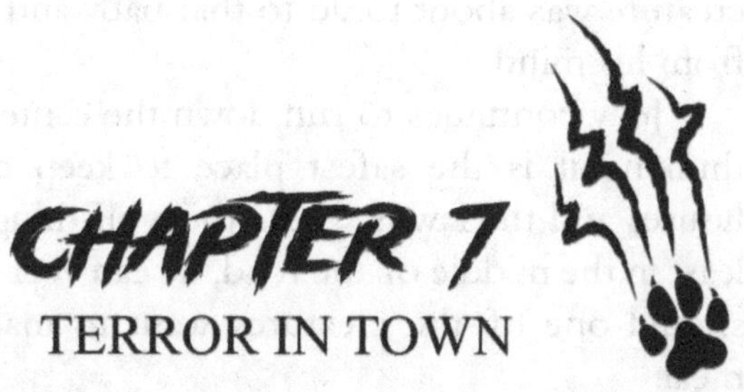

CHAPTER 7
TERROR IN TOWN

Joey hightails it through the darkening Talbotsville streets, which turned from his previous *Population: boring* comment into a war zone. His gaze darts and pans faster than he can control it, beholding the chaos and fiasco of his hometown. The city seems alive tonight, with residents screaming and running from wolf creatures.

Joey now holds his camera so it won't flop around as he runs. He passes a house with an opened attached garage. The overhead lights highlight a man wearing a red sweatband and tank top, curling dumbbells, with sweat dripping off his brows, while he watches the carnage outside. Joey grimaces when a wolf creature storms the garage, clasps its furry paws around the muscle man's throat, and lifts him off his feet. The last Joey sees as he turns to beat feet is a stream of blood fall from the bodybuilder's neck and douse his sneakers in crimson.

From Joey's left, a wolf creature wearing a torn plaid shirt galloped past, ignoring Joey altogether. While Joey ran, he thought that seemed odd—as he was a sitting duck out here—but he needed to get to Brad's. Then he understood why that creature had passed him over. The wolf-thing had a sleeping baby cradled in its arms and a teddy bear dangling from a paw. Joey refused to let himself think about what the creature was about to do to that baby and pushed the image from his mind.

Joey continues to run down the center line of the road, thinking it is the safest place to keep distance from the houses and the lawns where the wolf-things are invading. At least in the middle of the road, he can veer either left or right, should one of the creatures want to make him their next meal.

A parked Jeep's driver-side door opens ahead of Joey, and a punk kid wearing a black Scully cap slides from the seat to confront a wolf-thing that blocks his path. The kid recoils a fist to strike the creature's snout, but the furry paw takes one decisive uppercut swing, sending the kid stumbling backward into his Jeep. The wolf-thing closes the vehicle's door, and Joey watches it feed on the punk's neck through the open window. When the wolf-thing finishes, it meanders away, leaving blood dripping from the dead kid's neck and down the vehicle's door.

Joey rounds the corner and notices a wolf-thing hurdling the railing to someone's wraparound porch. Joey sees Brad's front steps just a bit down the street. A few more houses and Joey will be safe inside his brother's house. A few more houses without the horde of wolf-thing creatures noticing him…

When Joey reaches his brother's house, he bangs repeatedly on the front door but does not yell—not wanting to attract unnecessary attention to the house.

The door opens, and a hand reaches through to grab Joey's shirt and yanks him inside. Brad closes the door, panting, then pulls aside the curtain to the sidelight window to survey his curtilage. "Did they see you come here? Did they follow you?" Brad's questions come out as one syllable.

Joey shakes his head.

"What were you thinking? Being out there like that?" Brad scolds his younger brother. "These things have taken over the town! I even made Barbara leave to stay with her aunt in Parkview."

Joey frees his camera from around his neck. "I have something to show you." He points to the fur and blood still stuck to his camera. "And the roll of film in here contains pictures of one of the creatures hunting me at Landis Lake. It's all proof that we need to give to the cops."

Brad grabs Joey's shoulders to spin his little brother to look through the window at the pack roaming the streets and killing anything in their way. "Do you really think we need *proof* anymore?"

Joey adjusts his glasses on his nose. "I guess not." He spins to face his brother, with a hopeful grin. "But I know someone who can analyze this blood and hair and maybe can tell us what we are dealing with."

"Follow me." Brad leads Joey through the house and onto the sunporch off the kitchen. He gestures for Joey to sit at the card table, and he takes the seat next to his brother.

On the table sits a book titled *The Book of Werewolves: Being an Account of a Terrible Superstition* by Sabine Baring-Gould. Brad opens it and reads a few passages, reviewing the generic folklore of the werewolf mythos: must be killed by silver bullets, mostly feeds on the blood of animals, only transforms during a full moon, and must be genetically born as a werewolf.

Contrary to popular belief, the book was pretty adamant that real werewolves can't be transformed from the bite of another werewolf; yet the vampiric legend solely owns that literary device.

"Brad, you gotta level with me." Joey swallows hard. "Are we really talking about werewolves?"

"No, Joey." Brad closes the book and crosses his arms. "This is worse than werewolves."

Joey's eyes widen, and his mouth slackens. "What's worse than werewolves?"

Brad stands so fast that his chair tips over backward and clatters on the floor. "I dunno, but none of these creatures out there seem to follow any of the werewolf rules."

Joey again inspects the blood and fur stuck to the side of his camera. "We need to see Dr. Phyllis Pottinger, a professor at my college. That's who I meant when I said I know someone who can analyze the blood and fur and maybe tell us what we are really dealing with."

"Your college is four hours away. I don't know if Talbotsville can last that long."

As if on cue, sirens wail in the distance. Again Joey remains unsure if it is police, fire, ambulance, or a nuclear war siren. He just can't decipher between the different tones. "We need to leave it in the hands of the authorities right now, Brad. Let them hold down the fort while we get scientific answers to help defeat these beasts."

Brad nods. "We'll need to borrow my neighbor's car. I had to tow mine today. Busted radiator. And our folks are still out of town on vacation."

"What are we waiting for?" Joey jumps to his feet and follows Brad through the house and out the front door.

The brothers pause to survey the area for any immediate furry threats. When the coast is clear, they run across the lawn and onto Brad's neighbor's front porch.

Brad rings the bell, and they wait.

And wait.

And wait.

Brad eyes Joey, then peeks into the driveway. "Mr. Wilson's car is still here. He must be home. C'mon. Let's go through the back door. He leaves a key hidden under a rock for me, when I have to housesit his cats."

Joey nods in approval. The brothers beeline down the driveway and past Mr. Wilson's 1979 Ford Country Squire—wood paneling and all. Brad retrieves the spare key and unlocks the back door. The brothers carefully enter the well-lit house, the TV blaring an episode of *Family Ties* from the front room, and two cats jettison into hiding.

"Mr. Wilson?" Brad calls out.

No response.

The brothers inch through the house, checking each room for the old man. As they get closer to the room with the sounds of Michael J. Fox's straight-man comedic delivery and canned applause coming from the TV, Joey spots two legs on the floor. He taps his brother's shoulder and points down the hallway.

Brad crouch-runs toward his neighbor lying on the floor, today's daily newspaper discarded on the floor next to him. "Mr. Wilson, are you okay?" He shakes the old man with no response.

"Is he...?" Joey asks.

Brad regards his brother. "I think so."

"What could it have been? I don't see any wounds."

Brad chews on the inside of his cheek. "Maybe a heart attack?"

Joey's gaze draws an invisible line from Mr. Wilson's body to the front door. "Maybe he saw something that scared him to death?"

Brad notices Joey's focus on the door and approaches it. He closes one eye and leans toward the peephole. A wolf creature fills the entirety of his view, and it growls and bares its fangs at Brad. He stumbles backward, almost tripping over Mr. Wilson's legs, and spins to face Joey. "I think you're right. One of those beasts is on his front porch right now. One must have been here earlier too, when he looked out the peephole."

"We're lucky it didn't see us a few minutes ago when we were out there also. Do you know where he keeps his car keys?"

Brad snatches a ring of keys from a peg next to the front door. "I drive. You navigate."

Joey nods, and they run out the back door toward Mr. Wilson's car in the driveway.

Igor Cromwell Smith

Brian Paone: I would like to highlight the scene after Joey leaves Landis Lake and runs through town, while Howlers everywhere attack the residents. Everybody's accent is very nonregional. So, would you say Director Sampson was going for the feeling that this film takes place in Anywhere, USA?

Igor Cromwell Smith: When we storyboarded for a scene of this magnitude, we required 129 adult human extras, while using approximately nineteen children and forty-one wolves. We have an office in Baltimore and one just outside Boston. We got a lot of reception for this film. As an accent coach, my job is to strip away the annunciation in their vowels and their regional pronunciation so they sound like they could come from wherever in the country the film takes place.

BP: Did you have to work with any of the actors after they turned into Howlers so their howling sounded more authentic?

ICS: Well, that's an interesting question. When one is looking to hear a Howler, the howl is a very pronounced *oooowwww*. When I dealt with some of the extras, I would get an *oooohhhh* or an *aaaaaahhhhh*. There was a very distinct influx. Wally Sampson was very particular in the sound the Howler should make.

BP: Was it difficult to get all those costumed actors to howl in the same tone? Or was any of that overdubbed in post-production?

ICS: In this case, we had a wonderful voice actor. We used strictly his voice because, upon review, no one could quite hit the desired Howler tone. For most of the howls in the movie, if not 98.3 percent of them, all are from this one actor, who I shall not name, as he wishes to remain anonymous.

BP: So, you're telling me, when we watch this beloved childhood movie, all the Howlers' sounds are from the same actor voice, overdubbed?

ICS: Yes. A very classically trained voice actor, who eventually became prolific in the 1990s, provided all the howls from the Howlers.

BP: How do you feel that you just ruined a whole bunch of people's childhoods?

ICS: It should not surprise anyone, with Hollywood magic, how they do things. This actor trained gruelingly to nail the perfect howl, just once. He is one of the best in the business. It's just sheer talent.

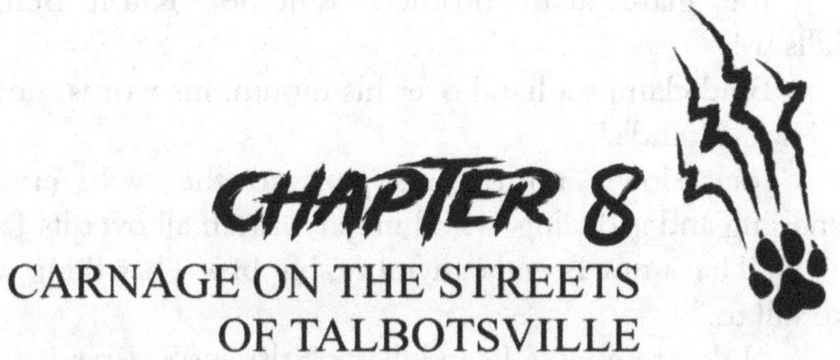

CHAPTER 8
CARNAGE ON THE STREETS OF TALBOTSVILLE

Brad puts Mr. Wilson's Country Squire in Reverse, rolls out of the driveway, and lumbers the car forward onto the roadway.

Joey remains silent as they cruise through the center of town. Flames from exploding vehicles reflect off the borrowed car's closed windows. Joey flinches when a wolf-thing tosses a lifeless body across the hood of the car.

Men, women, and children scream, running through the streets, over lawns, or out their front doors. Grunts and roars and howls litter the night air.

Chaos gives birth to more chaos. Frenzy becomes more frantic.

As Brad slams on the brakes, Joey throws out a hand against the dashboard to prevent himself from flying into the windshield.

Then Brad just sits here, the car idling.

It takes Joey a moment to collect himself from the abrupt halt and to notice a wolf-thing standing in front of the car—a wolf-thing with a very familiar yellow blouse. The car's headlights are like vertical pillars, framing the creature between.

"Brad," Joey whispers, "are you gonna run it over?"

"I–I can't." Brad's knuckles whiten with his grip on the steering wheel.

Joey glares at his brother. "Why not? Kill it. Before it kills us!"

Brad clamps a hand over his mouth, his words muffled. "That's Brenda."

Joey slowly returns his gaze to the wolf creature, snarling and growling, with hunger written all over its face.

"That's not Brenda anymore, big bro. That thing wants to kill us."

"I don't know if I can kill my girlfriend's sister."

The brothers flinch when a house explodes to their right, sending roof shingles and siding sky-high, and a fireball plumes into a mushroom cloud of black smoke.

"We gotta get out here! We gotta get answers or our town is doomed!" Joey yells.

Brad purses his lips, presses his chin against his chest to look forward from just beneath his eyebrows, and yells a war cry as he mashes the gas pedal. The Brenda-Wolf-thing raises its arms in a crisscross in front of its face just as the car strikes her.

Joey closes his eyes, unable to look at his brother—doesn't want to see what pained emotions are etched on his face—as he feels the Brenda-Wolf creature thump underneath the car's tires.

Brad glances in the rearview mirror as they exit Talbotsville, Brenda's transformed and furry body lying lifeless in the roadway behind them. He mashes the brake pedal, and the car screeches to a stop.

"What the…?" Joey eyes his brother.

Without answering, Brad flings open the car door and jogs to Brenda-Wolf's mangled body.

Joey leans sideways so he can see Brad and Brenda-Wolf in the car's side mirror. He grimaces when his brother bends down, places a kiss on the beast's bloody snout, and closes its eyelids with his hand.

Joey vows he will never mention what he just watched his brother do for as long as he lives.

Heidi Yawnson

Brian Paone: I would assume one of the most difficult scenes to shoot, as the lighting technician, is when Joey and Brad are in the car at nighttime, headlights on, and they run over the Brenda-Howler. The camera pans from the interior of the car to the exterior with the headlights. What were the tricks of the trade to get that scene so perfectly creepy?

Heidi Yawnson: Aluminum foil. You would be surprised how well that reflects just enough while being dampening enough to not wash out your subject.

BP: Director of Photography Juan O'Malley and I discussed how only one camera was available for the entire shooting of this movie. What were the obstacles to light, relight, to set up a new camera angle, to take down the camera, and repeat? Or did you do one establishing shot for each angle and edit it post-production?

HY: We filmed multiple takes from the garage interior, where we could control the exterior lighting. We used three flashlights and the interior lighting to balance out so the actors' faces were illuminated. When we filmed the street scene, we had to work with the ambient lighting from the streetlights. Things got a little dicey. Wally

Sampson insisted that we film the scene chronologically. This was something several people butted heads with. Ultimately, it's the way that we went with it. We had a crew in the trunk of the car. They would emerge from the trunk, remove the lighting. Then we would move the car a few feet and reshoot. Afterward, everyone would climb back into the trunk to not be in the background of the interior shots.

BP: The actress who plays the Brenda and Barbara twins, Academy Award Nominee Jennipher Johns, was very claustrophobic and anxiety-ridden when she was in the makeup. Some of your lights melted the latex onto her skin, and she had an infamous panic attack on set, where she swung at you and broke some of your gear. Do you wish to set the record straight on that incident?

HY: I don't think it's my place to say because she did have, what I guess we would call today, a nervous breakdown. Poor thing. She couldn't handle the bright hot lights. But that's stardom for you. If you want to be in the spotlight, well, that's showbiz for you.

CHAPTER 9
RESEARCH AND DISMEMBERMENT

Brad veers the Country Squire into the Scott Howard University parking lot, in front of the science wing.

"Why would she be here this late?" Brad asks Joey as they exit the car.

"She always stays late in the lab, furthering her research," Joey answers with a lightness to his tone.

Brad squints at his brother. "It sounds like you might have a thing for the good doctor."

Joey blushes. "Me? Golly gee no. Sheesh. Plus, if we survive this, I might have a date waiting for me."

"Oh?" Brad shoots Joey a grin. "You'll have to tell me about her when this is all over." Then his face becomes solemn. "I'll miss Brenda. I can't believe I had to kill her like that."

"We can grieve those we lost later." Joey wiggles his camera to punctuate his point. "Right now, we must save the town."

The brothers traipse through the sparsely occupied lot and through the glass doors. Brad follows Joey up two flights of stairs and down a corridor to a closed door adorned with a gold-colored nameplate that reads Dr. Phyllis Pottinger.

Joey knocks and waits for an invite inside. Hearing the go-ahead, Joey pushes open the door to reveal a redheaded woman in a white lab coat, bebopping from Bunsen burner to test tubes and back to a notebook.

"Hey, Joey. What are you doing here at this time of night?"

"Sorry to bother you, Doctor, but have you heard on the news what's happening to my hometown?"

Dr. Pottinger puts her mechanical pencil on her desk and places a hand on her hip. "Can't say I have."

"I think we need your expertise," Joey adds. "This is my brother Brad. It all started when his girlfriend's sister went missing a few nights ago…"

After Joey finishes recounting the events leading to them arriving at the university tonight, Dr. Pottinger slips a monocle onto her nose and, with a pair of tweezers, carefully scrapes the blood and fur from Joey's camera. She transfers the specimens onto a slide and slips it underneath a microscope on her desk.

"Doctor, with all due respect," Brad starts, "I know it sounds like we are dealing with werewolves on paper, but I think it's something beyond sinister."

The doctor removes the monocle, closes one eye, and uses the open one to inspect the slide's contents. The room falls silent, the brothers waiting with bated breath to hear what the scientist might find under the microscope.

Dr. Pottinger releases a low "*Uh-huh*," as if agreeing with someone in the room. She pulls her eye from the apparatus, sighs, and folds her hands into her lap. "Well, like Brad hypothesized, it's not werewolves."

Brad slaps Joey's chest. "See? Told ya." Then he faces the doctor. "It's worse than werewolves, isn't it?"

Dr. Pottinger rises and approaches a blackboard at the rear wall. She grabs a thick piece of white chalk and draws some elements of the periodic table, a DNA sequence strand, a crude sketch of a wolf, and a list of nouns.

Silver and *Super Blood Moon* are all Joey can discern before her quick handwriting becomes sloppy and makes the letters undecipherable.

She huffs out a long sigh and tucks a wayward strand of red hair into her ponytail. "Yes, it's worse than werewolves," Dr. Pottinger finally answers. "More insidious."

"Will someone just answer the question and tell me what is worse than werewolves?" Joey pleads with a huff.

Dr. Pottinger turns to glare at each of the brothers in turn. "Howlers! Howlers are worse than werewolves."

Joey furrows his brows and side-eyes Brad. "What in tarnation is a Howler?"

"Not a *what*," Dr. Pottinger corrects, "but a *who*."

"I don't follow," Brad says.

The doctor returns to the desk with the microscope and sits in a chair with a wheel at the bottom of each leg. "Howlers are always in beast form, unlike werewolves, who transmorph back-and-forth from human beings to wolf constructs."

"So, once they become wolflike, they never return to their human form?" Brad asks.

Joey knows his brother needs one more confirmation that killing his girlfriend's sister was not futile, that she will never be the Brenda who Brad knew nor the Brenda who Barbara loved.

"Correct," the doctor answers. "Once a Howler, always a Howler. And because of that, they don't need a full moon to have any special powers. However, the caveat to that rule is that Howlers tend to have heightened strength and senses during a super blood moon."

Brad eyes his brother. "For fuck's sake, tomorrow night is a super blood moon!"

"How do you even *know* that?" Joey asks, perplexed.

"The calendar in my kitchen has the moon cycles."

Joey nods, thinking how that tracks for his brother's love of all things celestial.

"Howlers are also highly intelligent," Doctor Pottinger adds. "They travel in packs from town to town, killing and feeding on some to satiate their thirst for blood, yet turning others into more Howlers to grow their numbers. And, even though they are immune to traditional weaponry, silver is their only known weakness."

"Can you be sure of that?" Joey asks. "If we're going back home to face these beasts, we can't be armed with misinformation that might get us and a lot of others killed."

"Or worse," Brad interrupts, "turned into a Howler."

"Right, big bro," Joey agrees.

Dr. Pottinger spins the microscope so it faces the brothers. "Take a peek in here, and I'll prove it."

Joey goes first and closes one eye so the other eye can focus. He watches oval blood molecules swim around on the slide. "It's still alive?"

"Very much so. A Howler's blood doesn't stop living until silver touches it. Keep watching."

Joey sees the tip of a small tweezer enter the slide from the direction where Dr. Pottinger stands, and, when the tweezer opens, a slice of silver hits the blood splatter. The molecules go crazy, smashing into each other like they are slam-dancing at a punk rock show. Then they vibrate, as if electrocuted, before each *pop, pop, pops*, like water balloons.

Joey lifts his head to face his brother. He mouths, *Oh my God*.

Brad takes a turn watching the exploding blood molecules at the hand of silver shards under the slide. He pulls back from the desk and nods once. "We should go home and try to get some sleep to prepare for the super blood moon tomorrow night."

"Thank you, Doctor." Joey shakes the scientist's hand.

"Be safe, boys. And godspeed."

Brad smiles at her, and the brothers head for the door. Joey opens it and enters the hallway.

Brad walks through the doorway, then pauses to turn back to regard the doctor one more time. "Ma'am, how do you know so much about the Howlers anyway? I've never heard of them before."

Dr. Pottinger sucks in her lips and stares at her shoes. "I made an oath to myself years ago after a Howler mauled my mother outside a butcher shop."

Brad's shoulders slump in empathy; he knows what losing someone to these monstrosities feels like. "Don't you want to come with us to help save the town, if it's so personal to you too?"

"Oh, child"—Dr. Pottinger puts a hand on Brad's arm—"I did just help you save the town, with the knowledge and information you gained here tonight."

"Some superheroes don't wear capes, Dr. Pottinger!" Joey calls out from the hallway.

"Be safe, boys. And rip apart a Howler for me," she says before closing the door, leaving the brothers to return to the war zone, now armed with a wealth of insight on how to stop these Howlers.

Ricky O'Reilly

Brian Paone: You are the world-leading werewolfologist on the werewolf mythos. Please tell us your name because Director Sampson did not include you in the end credits, which is a shame.

Richard O'Reilly: Slicky Dickey is my nickname, and werewolves are my game. There's a reason why I'm not in the credits. That's a real good reason.

BP: I had a hard time finding out who you were because of your missing name in the credits, but you were so integral to the world-building legend of the Howlers' characteristics. You have never told your story because no one, until this interview, knew who was behind the character development.

RO'R: Well, what do you want to know? Do you want a… [Taps bottom lip with his finger, while thinking] Let's see. I was born in 1956. My mother was a clerk, and my father molded steel and iron at the ironworks. What else are you looking for, sir? I don't know what you need.

BP: Why did Director Sampson omit your name from the credits?

RO'R: Well, you see, it all comes down to, sometimes folks just want you for your expertise. Other times they're just looking for some advice. And other times they just want a friend. Does that warrant some fancy treatment or written acknowledgment on a list of names that no one reads anyway?

BP: Director Sampson used your bottomless wealth of knowledge on all things werewolf because he wanted to create a different breed of cryptid that broke the mold on generic monster-movie rules. Almost all the tips and rules that Dr. Phyllis Pottinger, played by the talented Michelle Butts, gives Joey and Brad about the Howlers, came from you. I found them almost verbatim in your old interviews and very famous lectures from the 1970s and early 1980s. Do you think Sampson plagiarized some of your ideas? And that's why you're not listed as working on the film?

RO'R: As an expert on all things lycanthropic, I fancy myself, as you said, a werewolfologist. Self-proclaimed. I know it's all about creating different werewolf types. Are they ones that change with the full moon? Are they the ones with an aversion to silver? Some writers actually used my further research for a film series called *Underworld*, where the people could just turn into a werewolf. But I fancy the anomalies of the Howler myself, personally.

BP: Did you go through many iterations of what was lethal to the Howlers?

RO'R: I wrote a lot of things, some of which Wally used, but he was most interested in what would make a werewolf react negatively. And I said, *Shit, well, silver.* Obviously. Every few days, Wally Sanford would call me for more tips.

BP: Sampson.

RO'R: Sanford would ask me questions, like, "Where would the hair grow in at?" And I would say it would start at the muzzle. But then he asked me if a muzzle would be first during their transformation. Absolutely not. Any lycanthropic expert knows the muzzle comes in last. Of course the fangs are first, followed by the claws second. And, you know, the adjustment of the spine is next. We could be here all day.

BP: Did Director Sampson ever invite you on set during the filming?

RO'R: No. The special effects boys called me one time to adjust the claws, but they didn't bring me to a set but to a street. They didn't have any cameras. They didn't have any of the typical, what I would perceive to be, Hollywoody equipment, if you dig.

BP: I dig. What is your opinion of *Howlers* as a film and knowing you were essential to its cult status?

RO'R: I love any kind of a werewolf. I'm all about them, you know? So whenever I watch any of the movies from the 1980s and 1990s, I see how it all comes back to me and my research. And they're still making werewolf movies to this day. My grandmama used to always tell me, "Richie, Richie, you need to know about these, these Howlers," like they were real, you know? And then she would tell me that even something as simple as silverware could take them out. I could go into the cupboard for the china—but not, you don't want to take out *good* china, because Grandmama, she would give you all a whooping; you don't want none of that—so you go in there, and you get that silverware when she doesn't know. Oh, there better damn sure be a Howler outside. You better be damn sure before you start throwing your grandmama's silverware everywhere. You better hope you got knives. If you ain't got a knife, you get a fork. If not, in a pinch, a spoon could work, but you better be determined and damn sure ready to fight a werewolf. However, if it's a Howler, shit, you better count your days, my man, count your days.

CHAPTER 10
THIS'LL BE UZI

Brad and Joey returned to Talbotsville from Scott Howard University as the sun rose. After they surveyed the damage from the Howlers' nighttime onslaught on the town, the brothers agreed to get a good night's sleep during the daytime so they are well-rested both physically and mentally in preparation for tonight's super blood moon and what atrocities it may bring.

Brad's alarm clock buzzes and screeches to signal 4:00 p.m. Brad slams his palm on the alarm's snooze button to silence its cry and falls back asleep.

Brad sits upright in a panic and checks the clock. He slept another three hours. "Fuck," he mutters to himself, not knowing how many more people died due to his additional nap past their agreed-upon time of waking up.

Brad picks up the phone on his night table, dials his parents' phone number, where Joey is staying, and listens to the ringing, until his brother answers. "Hey, Joey. It's Brad. Sorry to call so late," he says groggily.

If Joey is mad at him for oversleeping, he doesn't mention it but lets Brad keep talking. And why didn't Joey come to the house after the meeting time passed? Maybe Joey overslept too...

"We gotta do something," Brad says, implying they need more than just the two of them to wage war on the Howlers. "Remember that guy who lived near Mom and Dad? That military guy? Kinda crazy? I think we should go see him. I'll be over in ten."

Brad holds the refrigerator door open while he peruses his parents' choice of soda. He shakes his head when he can't find a Jolt and settles for a can of Tab instead. He'll have to suggest that his parents go food shopping for some good drinks when they return from vacation.

Brad walks through the house and into the dining room, where their parents' old neighbor, Sgt. Auto Van Hellsing, leans over a crudely drawn map of Talbotsville resting on the table. A row of six grenades sits just above the map, and the rest of the tabletop contains an Uzi, a pistol, a revolver, a sheathed machete, and a samurai sword.

Sgt. Auto Van Hellsing straightens his posture when Brad enters the room. The veteran is the epitome of a doomsday prepper, wearing a marine-issued green undershirt, with two dog tags dangling from a silver chain around his neck. He has an ammunition belt full of Uzi rounds wrapping from his shoulder across his chest and under the opposite armpit. He has a freshly shaved head but a two-day-old beard, plus a cigar just barely hangs from his mouth.

Brad pops the top of his can of Tab and takes a long swallow.

Sgt. Auto Van Hellsing glares at Brad, as if to let Brad know the urgency of what is at stake and how drinking a soda has no place in that plan. To send his point home about the weight of the situation, Sgt. Auto Van Hellsing pulls a small mirror from his tactical pants' pocket and black camo face paint from another pocket. Holding the mirror to his face with one hand, he uses his other hand to apply the war paint under each eye.

Brad snickers under his breath, thinking the dude looks more like he is about to run routes and catch touchdowns than hunt some Howlers.

"Okay, boys. Huddle up!" Sgt. Auto Van Hellsing orders. "A plague has overtaken the town in the form of these werewolf freaks."

"Um, Auto… we learned they are not technically werewolves," Joey squeaks out, apprehensive to interrupt the start of the marine's inspirational speech. "They're called Howlers."

Sgt. Auto Van Hellsing waves Joey off, like he is an annoying mosquito, and ignores the interruption. "The pack has clustered in the neighborhoods around the area, with a few offshoots down near Landis Lake and some by the zoo." He slams his index finger at each location on the hand-drawn map in front of him as he lists off the spots. "Probably trying to crossbreed with some of the animals."

"Yeah… no. Hi," Joey interrupts again. "So, it doesn't work that way. Dr. Pottinger said the Howlers make more of their kind by transforming humans, not breeding."

Sgt. Auto Van Hellsing rips the cigar from his mouth, ash falling onto where the lake is portrayed on the map, and glares at Joey. "So, the church over here, looking real good." He points to the church by memory and without removing the intense eye contact with Joey, then he refocuses on the paper below him and points to each location in turn. "And we've got the north, east, west up here. We're gonna take the road way up there. And kill them Howlers."

Joey smiles when Sgt. Auto Van Hellsing corrects himself regarding the beasts' moniker.

"And we're gonna take these grenades and shove them right up their Howler butts." Sgt. Auto Van Hellsing grabs two grenades from the table. "And then we're gonna come back to the house for a lil cake and ice cream."

Joey furrows his brows at Brad, silently questioning what cake and ice cream had anything to do with tonight's super blood moon fight.

Brad shrugs and takes another sip of his Tab.

"We gotta be careful though," the marine shares. "These things are experts in the art of killing! And they're smart! But you know what they're not as smart as? A US military-trained human being with a gun! So grab a weapon, boys."

"Auto?" Joey interrupts again, rubbing his eyebrow to redirect his nervous energy anywhere except for making eye contact with the marine. "Dr. Pottinger made it very clear that silver is their only weakness, so unless your Uzi shoots silver bullets, I would advise you to rethink your—"

"It's time to hunt some Howlers. *Oorah!*" the marine yells, as if Joey never spoke at all. Auto grabs the pistol from the table and slips it into a drop-down holster on his leg, then manhandles the Uzi. His final touch of preparation is to jam his lit cigar into his mouth and puff while he waits for the Bradshaw brothers to pick their weapons.

Brad shoots Joey a *What are ya gonna do?* look and unsheathes the machete as his choice, while Joey grabs the revolver.

"Let's go, boys!" Sgt. Auto Van Hellsing exclaims and opens the front door to lead the brothers into battle.

The super blood moon hangs low in the sky, illuminating Talbotsville like it was noontime.

Sgt. Auto Van Hellsing runs down the walkway from the front door, pivots to his left, and squeezes the Uzi's trigger.

The brothers watch only a handful of rounds fire, before a Howler appears from where Sgt. Auto Van Hellsing is shooting. The Howler, unscathed, leaps onto the marine's chest. Sgt. Auto Van Hellsing falls backward, the Uzi still firing but into the moonlit sky now, as the Howler mauls his neck, sending a spurt of blood like a fountain, lessening with each diminishing heartbeat... until the marine stops writhing and the blood stop spurting. And the Howler feeds on his newly acquired feast of Oorah flesh.

The brothers look at each other and scream, then hightail it back inside their parents' house and slam the door. Joey, revolver in hand, pulls back the white lace curtain from the thin sidelight window and grimaces as the Howler devours the man who was supposed to help retake the town.

Dirk Socks

Brian Paone: Dirk, it's nice to interview you again about your toy lines.

Dirk Socks: Nice to see you, Brian. Always a pleasure. Last time we met, we discussed… [gives quizzical look]

BP: Your Halloween masks for the *Sick Puppies* trilogy.

DS: *Ahh*, that's right. [Crosses legs and visibly relaxes] What a crazy series that was to work with. [Chortles] Parents just didn't understand the tongue-in-cheek satire of the *Sick Puppies* films. I blame them for the failed mask line. But *overcome, adapt, improvise*, am I right?

BP: You certainly did that after *Sick Puppies*. You owned one of the fastest-rising movie tie-in marketing companies in the world during the mid-1980s. You were ready to take down Mattel and all the big conglomerates. But one movie ruined your career. It's been a long road for you during these thirty-nine years that the movie has been out, but I want to go over some ideas you had that hit the shelves and some ideas that never made it past the planning stage. The first action figure you produced for the *Howlers* line was Sgt. Auto Van Hellsing because he closely resembled G.I. Joe, and you intended to rival the

G.I. Joe franchise by using a short-lived character from *Howlers* that was not a Howler.

DS: You got to think on your feet. You got to be quick, you know? When you're quick, you're thinking of all kinds of ideas. Mile a minute, mile a minute, mile a minute. You know what I'm saying? So, we had all kinds of ideas when this movie came out. When *Howlers* landed in my lap, I envisioned everything, like that Mel Brooks film where they pimp the merchandise. That was the idea. You got to hit the ground running. You can't stop. If you fall off your bike, you better get back on your legs and keep on running. Catch up to your bike. That's what you need to do. So, we had some ideas. We thought tee-shirts, hats, stickers, bumper stickers. We went into all kinds of stuff. Then we said, let's go deeper. I mentioned a bicycle. We had a *Howlers* bicycle. It was beautiful, had tassels on it. It was hot pink, yellow, and red. Lots of colors. You were bright. You could be seen any time of the day. Then we went deeper into some thoughts. We were in the boardroom, just throwing darts at a board. You just got to keep going, keep them ideas coming, keep them coming, keep them coming. That's what you got to do. You got to always be running, always be running, never stop, never stop. You stop, you're dead. That's how marketing works. You run out of ideas, you run out of steam, you die. You fizzle out. We came up with everything. Action figures, television shows, cartoon spinoffs. We even went as far as having the Atari 2600 adaptation of Howlers the Videogame. We were working on that. We had a small development team, who were making the marine figure as the main character. He actually picks up an assault rifle in the game, but we got in trouble because it resembled the Rambo version of the Atari game. It was very different, because we weren't fighting—What was Rambo fighting?—Commies? It doesn't matter. We were fighting Howlers. You want to know why the Sgt. Auto Van Hellsing figure failed? Poor design. The legs didn't move. The arms didn't move. You know what did move? The head. What good is it for a man to turn his head around, when he can't turn his arms and raise them? You can't hold a rifle like that.

BP [watching Dirk Socks take his first full breath]: I think the consumers reached a breaking point with the merchandise when Howler-themed mousetraps arrived in hardware stores. When did you feel you may have crossed the line with the *Howlers* swag?

DS: If there was a line, I damn sure was, dancing, just strutting right over it. I was fine with it. We were developing *Howlers* breakfast cereal, *Howlers* bedsheets, *Howlers* blenders. We had a deal with Bissell to produce steam cleaners for when your little pooch makes a mess in the house. We had everything. Always be thinking. Always be working. Always be creating. ABC, my man. ABC—Always Be Creating.

BP: We won't discuss the specifics surrounding that tragic accident involving a child and a *Howlers* squirt gun, but does the outcome of that incident still haunt you?

DS: Now, the *Howlers* squirt gun, that was… You know when you have a wrestling action figure, and you got your little Hulkamania Hogan? They'll always have a cheap Chinese, Japanese, South Korean knockoff. That's what happened with that situation. We never actually made a squirt gun. We had a prototype, and while what happened to that little boy is a tragedy, we can't be held responsible. Somebody stole our prototype, and a bootleg company massproduced it.

BP: The *Howlers* merchandise oversaturated the market and eventually disappeared from the shelves, after collecting dust for numerous holiday seasons, to make space for successful 1990s' movie toy lines. You were eventually fired, and you never worked in toy manufacturing again. What have you been doing the better part of thirty-nine or so years?

DS: Well, first off, it wasn't our fault that the toys didn't sell. We had a good product. It wasn't us who was wrong. It was the children who were wrong. They don't know good toys. Now you see them tap-tap-tapping away on their phones. I recently tried to relaunch my career with the *Howlers* app game because that's where the kids are at. I'm still an idea man. That's all I do. I come up with ideas. When one business folds, another door opens. Even if that door is to a Target. Maybe I work in the shoe department. Maybe I don't. I look at it as a footwear specialist. I'm not a shoe guy. I'm the footwear specialist. I stock the shelves. I tell you what shoe size you need to wear. That's where I'm at. I'm here to find you a good product. Always have been. Always will.

BP [after a few long blinks, trying to understand the last part of Dirk's answer]: Regarding non-toy film tie-ins and an example how timing is key, the time machine car from *Back to the Future* is a DeLorean. That company stopped producing them in 1982, then went out of business in '83. Some have speculated that, if they had survived long enough for *Back to the Future* to come out in '85, the DeLorean would have thrived, and we would maybe still have them in production. If you had held on long enough to bridge the gap between your toy company folding and the popularity of the sold-out midnight showings of *Howlers* every weekend all over the continent—backed with a shadow cast, like *Rocky Horror Picture Show*—years later, could you have salvaged the company by targeting the merch to those attendees instead of children?

DS: Who's to say? The videogame didn't take. It got buried in a landfill with the Atari 2600 E.T. game. The silverware didn't take. It fell apart. That's on the manufacturers though. Not on me. It was a great idea. It's a hell of a tie-in. That's all I'm about. Tie-ins. I'm about selling ties. Tie-ins. Maybe I sell ties now. Who cares?

BP: Have you attended any of these midnight screenings of *Howlers*? To packed houses, to people throwing silverware at the screen at certain parts of the movie, to people dressed as Howlers? Have you experienced the full immersion of fandom in a theater that they do now?

DS: Well, my idea train is always rolling. Always rolling. Keep it rolling. Like I say, you got to keep moving. Got to keep moving. When I noticed the midnight showings pop up, I had an idea, *ding, ding, ding*. You know what I'll do? I'll make shirts. So, I hopped online to order solid-color shirts and slapped on the *Howlers* logo. I stand outside as many theaters as I can and as often as I can to sell the shirts. It's all about making that money. All about making that buck and making the fans happy. And, if the fans are happy, I'm making money. And, if I'm making money, then I'm happy.

BP: I can tell you're chomping at the bit for me to ask this final question because you're excited to announce some big news to the fans that we discussed before I turned on the microphone.

DS: [Rapidly taps foot, shifts anxiously in the chair]

BP: Tell everybody what is opening on Christmas next year that you singlehandedly put together.

DS [Smiles]: Oh boy, *Howlers* the musical on Broadway! This has been an idea I've been trying to sell since 1994. I pitched the idea originally to Stephen Sondheim who, to say he walked out would be an understatement. I've never seen someone run so fast. We pitched it to several prolific writers, these playwrights who, you know, they're big names. Their names sell alone. They're the Stephen King of playwrights. They're the George Lucas of playwriting. They're the name that you go to. Nobody would take it. It took us years. I started to feel like Kermit the Frog in *The Muppets Take Manhattan*. Now here we are. I'm happy to say we're in serious negotiations with Hugh Jackman to play Brad. We haven't heard back, but I think it's safe to say that, yes, we might. But I'm excited. Are you excited? Because I'm excited.

BP: I'm excited. Yes.

DS: You going to get a ticket?

BP [Chuckling]: Am I on the guest list?

DS: No, but I'll sell you a ticket right now. [Laughs]

BP: The fans adore the original score and theme song, written and performed by Hiphopmcdougal, but they didn't want to contribute to the musical, so you contacted Andrew Lloyd Webber, who also declined.

Can you reveal who you signed to write the songs for *Howlers: the Musical?* Because it's going to be big.

DS: Well, I guess the wolf's out of the bag. If anybody is hearing this… Will there be audio of this interview? Is this for a radio show? What is, what is this?

BP: No, this will be transcribed for the thirty-ninth anniversary of the film's novelization.

DS: A gentleman by the name of Christian Jacobs, from the band called the Aquabats, is writing the whole thing. He's a very serious songwriter, and I think he'll bring something unique to the table. [Looks to the side, as if he expected a video camera] So bring your forks and bring your loved ones—Broadway, Christmas next year!

CHAPTER 11
HI-YO, SILVERWARE! AWAY!

"We're on our own," Joey murmurs. "I can't believe Auto was taken out that fast. If the super blood moon is making the Howlers that much stronger, where they can kill a survivalist like Sgt. Auto Van Hellsing so easily, then what chance do we have, Brad?" His voice rises in volume. "Tell me, what chance do we have? He didn't even last twenty seconds out there. How are we gonna last twenty minutes—"

Brad slaps his brother across the cheek. "Snap out of it, dude! Dr. Pottinger said the only way to kill them is with silver. It's not our fault that Captain America out there didn't heed our advice. Yet we can. We can give these fuckers exactly what the doctor ordered! Literally."

"I got it. You didn't have to add *literally*," Joey says. "That was like explaining the punchline to a joke."

"I'll punchline your joke, lil bro. Come here." Brad grabs Joey into a brotherly bear hug and gives him a noogie. "We're gonna be triumphant tonight. We can't let down Brenda and all the other turned Howlers. Their deaths can't be in vain."

"Right!" Joey says, rejuvenated. "Where are we going to find real silver?"

Brad looks ceilingward. "In the attic."

"Do you mean…?"

"Yes. Grandma's old silver utensils."

"Mom and Dad will kill us!" Joey protests.

Brad grabs his brother's shirt and balls the fabric in his fist. "And, if we don't act, those Howlers might kill Mom and Dad before they can get to us."

"Good point."

They take off running up the stairs and pull the drawstring that lowers the flush attic door from the ceiling. The stairs unfold until the bottom step lands on the hallway floor. Brad goes first, Joey following behind. Finding the box marked GRANDMOTHER'S SILVER UTENSILS is easy; getting it down the skinny attic stairs is not.

Once in the dining room again, now with a box of vintage silver utensils among the scattered grenades and the samurai sword, Brad retrieves a hammer from the junk drawer. He grabs a dining room chair, flips it over, and smashes the hammer into two legs to remove them.

Joey crisscrosses his arms in front of his face to shield his eyes from any flying wooden shrapnel, and Brad pauses mid-swing, remembering how that is the same movement Brenda made before he ran her over with Mr. Wilson's car.

Brad shakes the image from his head and resumes beating the legs clean off the chairs.

"Are you crazy? What in Sam Hell are you doing?" Joey chastises.

Without answering, Brad proffers the broken chair leg, grabs a roll of duct tape from the junk drawer, and secures a knife at the end, like a bayonet. He jabs an invisible enemy in the corner of the room to demonstrate the weaponry.

"Genius," Joey murmurs. "Turns out we don't need fancy weapons. We just need silver."

"Now make yours, little brother. But just know, this means we'll have to get up close and personal to use them effectively. Are you ready for that? Are you up for the challenge?"

"I was fucking born ready!" Joey exclaims and rummages through the box of utensils, removes a fork, and extends his hand for the other broken chair leg.

As Joey wraps the duct tape around the fork and the end of the chair leg, they hear a symphony of howling in the distance. They glance toward the front door, and Brad glimpses Sgt. Auto Van Hellsing's partially eaten body through the window.

"But, Joey, I'm nervous." Brad sets his weapon on the hutch and places both palms on the dining room table. "I don't know if we can do this, man."

"Look. I know tonight has been the worst night of both of our lives," Joey stands a bit straighter. His hair a bit more in place.

Brad nods.

"Now, half the town may be dead. And the other half may be transformed into those Howlers. But we can end this."

Brad pushes himself from the table and stands a bit more confidently while listening to his brother's motivational speech.

"Here." Joey taps a finger on the table to punctuate his point. "Tonight. So that the next super blood moon won't mean impending doom."

Brad's nodding becomes more pronounced as his brother speaks, the words resonating deep within his soul.

"But, when the streets are free and clear and safe for the citizens to walk, it'll mean we were triumphant over these beasts from hell. So, grab your knife, Brad. And I'll grab my fork. And we'll finish this. Once and for all!"

Brad breathes out a "Yeah, we will!" and the Bradshaw brothers high-five just as the howling from outside grows closer.

Brian Paone: I'm here with the owner of PD Catering, Patty Simmons. You were in charge of providing all the food and drinks for the length of the shoot. Tell me how Director Sampson found your company originally among all the catering companies at the time?

Patty Simmons: Mr. Sampson said he had a mutual friend who used me before, and they recommended us to him. And, long story short, I wish they didn't.

BP: Why do you wish they didn't? Because, when this movie came out, and it became the summer blockbuster, I'm sure your catering company grew beyond anything you had expected. You probably couldn't handle the influx of new accounts. Stephen Spielberg called you to exclusively cater his movies. You had a waiting list for all the big names of the era. How was having the Hollywood moguls consider *you* the celebrity of catering companies?

PS: Honestly that sounds exciting from the outside, but, being on the inside, as the company owner, I regret all of it now. I offered upscale fine dining to my clients, and, for *Howlers*, we even took it up a notch. However, no matter how professional I was, the cast and crew were not so professional.

BP: Academy Award Nominee Jennipher Johns, who played the twins, Brenda and Barbara, carries a reputation of being hard to deal with on set. Did she give you any problems?

PS: Did she give me any problems? Boy, did she ever. [Chortles, with an eyeroll] She felt the need to stay in character as a Howler and stole my silverware. And she started throwing it. I felt like I was working at an animal shelter and that I was serving animals—or should I say *Howlers*—that had no idea how to use utensils at all. No matter how prestigious this Jennipher acts as a quote, unquote celebrity, I wouldn't say she's worth much.

BP: Wonderwolves Inc. brought dozens of wolves onto the set. Was your company also in charge of feeding the wolves?

PS: Yeah, we fed the wolves gourmet wet dog food, and honestly, they acted more humane than the humans. So that was surprising. I would definitely cater to the wolves again but not the actual people.

BP: Did Jennipher Johns stay in Howler character even while she ate?

PS: She never broke character.

BP: Did she ever fight the wolves for their food, like on the floor?

PS: Yeah. So, we frequently had to refill several wolves' bowls because she kept emptying them. And then we found utensils cracked in half. And I didn't even know you could do that with silverware. This is fine dining. I gave my best stuff to these people, and they just ruined it all. I felt like I was catering to savages.

CHAPTER 12
EVERY DOG HAS ITS DAY, EVERY WOLF WILL BE SLAYED

"All right, little brother," Brad says as he turns the doorknob and swings open the front door, "time for a little hand-to-paw combat. Let's do this!"

The Bradshaw brothers tactically descend the front steps, back-to-back, so they can see each other's sixes, utensil weapons raised at the ready.

A growl sounds before they see a Howler's furry arm and tattered suit jacket hidden by the large oak tree on the front lawn.

"Brad, one is behind the tree," Joey whispers.

Brad holds his knife-stick low against his hip and charges forward. The Howler spins from behind the tree trunk and, with one swipe, knocks the makeshift weapon from Brad's hands. Brad stumbles backward from the force and uses the distance between himself and the discarded utensil-spear and the proximity of the Howler to calculate that he has zero chance to retrieve the knife before the Howler can kill him.

"Grab the bat!" Joey yells.

Brad scans the grass and locates the abandoned baseball bat lying halfway in their parents' rose garden. The Howler makes its Howler sounds as it lunges forward but stops, almost taunting Brad to use the blunt sportsball equipment.

Brad crouches slowly, staring into the Howler's eyes but feeling for the bat. For a fleeting moment, he thinks he recognizes old man Zevon—a one-time local musical hero, now turned corporate nine-to-fiver. Brad chances a glimpse at the baseball bat now in his hands—PEACEKEEPER written in black Sharpie down the wooden barrel.

Brad rises from his crouch to a batter's stance, pulls the Peacekeeper back to his right shoulder, adjusts his grip on the handle, and when the old man Zevon–Howler reaches striking distance, Brad swings, batta-batta, swings... batta!

The tip of the bat strikes the Zevon–Howler in its left ear hard enough to send the beast staggering backward, then it falls on the lawn, motionless, a fountain of blood spurting from the gaping hole in its head.

Brad looks back at his brother with a triumphant grin and a thumbs-up. "I think we are gonna win this war tonight!"

"You have to pierce him with silver, or he'll get up again," Joey calls out. "It's the only way to truly kill them, remember?"

"Right!" Brad runs to collect his knife-stick and jams it into old man Zevon's stomach.

The Howler's eyes fling open, and it grabs the chair leg to try to dislodge the knife from its belly, but its strength diminishes right before Brad's eyes, until the Howler lies lifeless, its tongue hanging from its snout, like a dehydrated puppy.

Brad regards his brother with widened eyes and a dry mouth from realization. "Does that mean that... Brenda is still alive, even though we ran her over with the car? If we didn't use silver?"

Joey steps off the stoop, approaches his brother, and places a hand on Brad's shoulder. "Let's hope we don't have to find out."

Without warning, Joey charges toward something Brad didn't see in their parents' driveway and spears his utensil-bayonet into a Howler's chest that rounded the corner of the garage.

Brad surveys the street in front of them. "Do you think they can talk to each other telepathically, Joey?"

"I don't know. Why?"

"Because it looks like every Howler in existence is heading toward us for revenge. Look!" Brad's eyes widen in disbelief and horror.

Joey wonders if this is how the Bradshaw brothers finally meet their match—going down in a blaze of glory…

Brian Paone: Ken, the first thing I want to ask you is—

Ken Gunner: You ever been thrown out of a forty-seven-story window, son? I don't think so. The answer is no. I have. Continue.

BP [after a pause to collect myself]: Many *Howlers* fanatics want to know why Mr. Wilson needed a stunt double. After all, the old man's entire role consists of lying motionless on the floor after Joey and Brad figure out that he must have looked through the peephole and fell backward when a Howler startled him.

KG: What do you know about Hollywood, son? Do you know anything? Do I come into your office and ask you what that space bar is for? Do I do that? Do I ask you how a stapler works? Is this what you do? No, no, you don't, do you? Why are you going to come in here, into my home, and shit on my floor and tell me that it's caviar, *huh*? *Huh*? Don't sass me, boy.

BP: All right, Mr. Gunner. You eventually became very well-respected in Hollywood as a stunt coordinator, but I heard you were the twelfth pick for *Howlers* after they had already started shooting. What happened to the eleven before you?

KG: When Wally was shopping *Howlers*, I was still new to the game, a baby, new to the game. Well, let's see. I'm just trying to remember some of my predecessors. One guy got a shattered spine while completing the stunt that you just took a shit ride all over. Do you understand how intense some of these stunts are? For that man to fall on the floor after looking through the peephole? He shattered his spine—his *spine*. That man will never walk again. Then we had the scene where I do believe it was, it was a reporter character maybe. I don't remember.

BP: The main character? Joey Bradshaw?

KG: I just know that I was needed, and I had to oversee his stunt double to—

BP: Chad Waters played Joey, and he didn't have a stunt double. Joey's brother in the film, Brad, had one. Are you talking about Brad's stunt double, Elliot Platt? [If looks could kill me…]

KG: *Actor*s are not as classically trained in the physicality as we are. I didn't serve in Vietnam for you to come here and sass me, okay?

BP: Got it. So, did you find it harder to do the stunts with humans or with the Howlers?

KG: Now, are we talking about those people in the suits or the real dogs? Because them weird ones who dressed up like cats or dogs or whatever they were supposed to be, man, they were hard to work with. But they had some real dogs on set, and they were fine. I had no issues with them. They were trained. There was some, I don't know, some European, maybe an Italian fella or something.

BP: That was Hans from Wonderwolves Inc.

KG: He had them under control, let me tell you, him and his cohort. He yelled at them in some kind of language I didn't get.

BP: German. He speaks German.

KG: But, damn, those dogs listened.

BP: Wolves. There were no dogs on set.

KG: [His glare is like knives]

BP: On day three of shooting, Wally Sampson banned you from eating any of PD Catering's food because of an incident at breakfast that morning.

KG: He was mad because I took his coffee. You understand what I have to do, son? When I wake up in the morning, I shit excellence. I don't put my leg into my pants the way you do. When I do it, it's a miracle. It's miraculous. It's life changing. You can hear the thunder and the lightning crack when my feet go through those holes at the bottom of my jeans. You still do to this day. I might be in a walker. I might be wheeling myself around, but, by God, I'll still kick your ass. And just like that day when I took his coffee, I looked him in the eye, and I said, "What are you gonna do about it?" Well, I guess he decided to assert his dominance with some legalities and put a restraining order on me and said I couldn't even be on set for a whole seventy-two hours. And guess what? One of the actors stubbed their toe. And where was I? Not on set. Good. That's what I think. I wish he stubbed his other toe too.

BP: There's an iconic scene—and this image was used for Trapper Keeper covers throughout the rest of the 1980s—where a Howler, using only one paw, hurdles over someone's front porch railing. How dangerous was that stunt for the person in that costume?

KG: Well, for that shot, that was me in the costume. I did that stunt. I'm the quintessential coordinator, sure, but Sampson put me up front and center for that one. He put in Gunner. That's what I am. I'm the Gunner.

BP: This was obviously after the seventy-two-hour restraining order had expired.

KG: Shush, boy. I got myself all up in that doggy suit. It's all sweaty and gross. And they rigged me up. And they had the crane lift me up a little bit. And we went up and over that railing.

BP [My eyebrows raised]: Do you think Sampson was doing this only to get you back for drinking his coffee?

KG: Sampson is a piece of shit for sure, but he ain't a reckless piece of shit. It took, I want to say, a half-dozen shots to get it right. One time, I didn't even make it over. My foot caught on the railing. We had to reset the take. Can you imagine if an actor did that? They would have broken their whole leg, son.

BP [Squinting at him so he might hear his own words]: Maybe Sampson was ready to try his thirteenth choice…

KG [Pausing… eyes widen]: Sweet baby Jesus in a manger! That piece of shit *was* trying to get me hurt! Next question, before I find what trailer park he's living in this month and give him a good ole knuckle sandwich.

BP [Clearing throat] The opening scene, where Brenda is beating off the Howler—

KG: What kind of movie you watching, boy? That's called bestiality, son. You in a whole other kink.

BP [horrified yet trying not to laugh]: Let me rephrase that, sir. During the Brenda-versus-Howler fight scene in front of the zoo, she hits the Howler many times with her pocketbook. Was an actor inside the Howler costume, or was it a stunt double?

KG: What makes you think it would be the actor? They are too sissy to go ahead and take a pocketbook in the face—costume or not. You know how heavy those purses are? Them women carry everything in them things. Everything from their jewelry to money to hairbrushes to bricks. I had to sync it. Getting hit by that. That's no small feat.

BP: And the one thing I definitely want to touch on—

KG: I bet you do, Mr. Beating Off the Wolf. [Snorts]

BP: The end. That climax.

KG: That's what she said.

BP [Sighing heavily]: When the Howlers finally overrun the town, it appears on screen that hundreds of Howlers are attacking. Cars are on fire, and people and Howlers are rolling around with weapons, and it's just a melee. It's bedlam. It's a fiasco. All while Joey and Brad run through the town. Film schools discuss and dissect that scene every semester, regarding how to shoot such a chaotic scene in one take. Plus, that one scene clocks in at almost ten minutes of screen time. That was all filmed in one shot. There was no cut. Movie buffs will study that scene for generations to come. How stressful was it for you to know that, if one of your stuntmen messed up, Director

Sampson would call to reset all those extras and crew to restart from the very beginning of that scene.

KG: When you watch that scene, you've got to realize it wasn't just me. That is a monumental undertaking. We pulled in this lady who was just starting her career—this lady by the name of Paula Abdul. She coordinated what was basically a dance. And that's all choreography is. It's a dance, son. It's a dance. That's all it is. You punch me? I move to the left. You kick me? I move to the right. It's all a dance. It's a tango, baby. It's a tango. That's what it is.

BP: Would you say we could compare the end of that scene, if looked at through different eyes, to Michael Jackson's *Thriller* video?

KG: Maybe better? This scene… [He coughs until he clears his throat] This scene makes anything… [Another round of hacking] It makes Michael Jackson look like the worst dancer on the planet. It makes any choreographer in the world pale in comparison. This is a masterpiece. This is better than *The Nutcracker*.

BP: You have been publicly very critical about Michael Jackson's werewolf stunts in his *Thriller* video. If you had overseen the *Thriller* video, what would you have done differently for his werewolf character?

KG: First off, I would have been in the suit. I don't know why Mr. Jackson was in the suit. May he rest his soul. That could have killed him, doing those werewolf stunts. That's no joke. When he jumped out, when he turned around suddenly, he could have twisted his spine. He could have shattered a vertebra. And don't get me started about what genius thought it was a grand idea to let Michael J. Fox surf on *top* of a moving van for *Teen Wolf*. You're laughing at me. You don't understand.

BP: I'm sorry, Mr. Gunner. I'm laughing because that wasn't Michael J. Fox on top of the van in *Teen Wolf*. They most certainly used a stunt double.

KG [Looks over my shoulder in a thousand-mile stare, and I see and hear him swallow hard]: How do you think I got in this wheelchair? Coordinating stunts like that. [He mumbles to himself] On top of a moving van, my ass.

BP: Yes, but there's a silver lining in every cloud because, after your wheelchair incident, you became the world's renowned leader of Hollywood films when they need a stunt coordinator for a wheelchair-bound character. You're giving back to the medium, and it must feel good that you are still working, and you're helping handicapped actors perform super-dangerous stunts in some of these current blockbuster action films—even though you're stuck in a wheelchair, paralyzed.

KG: Well, when I got paralyzed on the set of *Howlers*, I thought my career was over. A couple years later, I got called up for some weird alien film. I got to use my wheelchair. They launched me off a cliff. I splashed into a lake. One of my best, best scenes of all time, but they didn't use my take. They got some able-bodied actor, but I think I gave the best take. But they use me as an example every time. So maybe I'm not giving the speeches they want? Maybe I'm telling them the way that I want it done? Maybe I go off on my socials too much. But they can't deny that I set the bar. I am the blueprint.

BP: Last question, Mr. Gunner. What was your fondest memory of working on *Howlers*?

KG: When the film ended.

CHAPTER 13

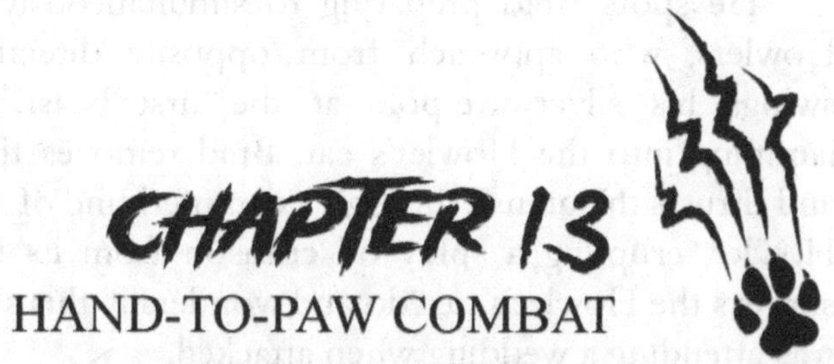

HAND-TO-PAW COMBAT

Joey scans the shadows across the street. Dozens of furry silhouettes shamble toward them. "Looks like they've sent up their Bat symbol to amass the troops to descend upon their exterminators. But we will not go softly into the night!"

"Right!"

"We will not let them take what's ours!"

"Preach, brother!"

Joey raises his fork-spear above his head. "We won't stop until we rid these hellhounds from our little slice of heaven!"

"Okay, Joey, I think everyone, including the Howlers, get your point."

The swarm of pointed-eared figures in the distance seem to have gotten bored with Joey's enthusiastic speech too because they now zoom across the street in a blur of fur at the brothers.

Joey spins and sends his fork-spear, like a javelin, through the air and across the front lawn, in a throw that would make any Olympic gold-medal recipient proud. Straight and true, the weapon's tines find their mark in a Howler's chest, and the beast falls backward, squirming and spitting blood. The youngest Bradshaw brother sprints toward the fallen Howler and yanks his weapon from the chest cavity, then spins on his heels, ready to eradicate another one of these beasts, He-Man style.

He spots Brad preparing to simultaneously fight two Howlers, who approach from opposite directions. Brad swings his silverware-pole at the first beast, the knife jamming into the Howler's ear. Brad removes the weapon and thrusts the utensil through a cummerbund of the second Howler, erupting a spray of crimson from its belly. Brad surveys the Howler's tuxedo and wonders if this slayed beast was attending a wedding when attacked.

Joey snaps from being mesmerized by his brother's ninja moves when a Howler's breath dots Joey's neck with warmth and moisture. Realizing he is too close to use his fork-spear, Joey plants his left foot and roundhouse kicks the Howler in his snout. The beast flails its arms as it skitters backward, where Joey finishes it off by ramming the silver utensil through the beast's cheeks and upward into its brain.

The Bradshaw brothers take a beat to catch their breaths, eye each other, and in silent reverence for one another, raise their fists, holding their respective weapons, and charge into the street.

Stab!

Splat!

Swing!

Spurt!

Swipe!

Shove!

Scrape!

Shuffle!

Stab!

Splat!

Smash!

Squeeze!

Scream!

Stare!

Shuffle!

Stab!
Splat!
Shake!
Squeeze!
Smother!
Stomp!
Scratch!
Shatter!
Slide!
Stab!
Splat!
Sniff!
Spin!
Shift!
Spear!
Stab!
Splat!
Stop!
And finally…
Smile!

The brothers stand, panting from exhaustion, and survey the dismembered Howlers littering the street and nearby front lawns.

"I don't see anymore," Brad says, bending over, his hands on his thighs, catching his breath. The streets are painted in blood and fur.

Joey wipes his cheek with the back of his hand, leaving a crimson smear across his face from all the entrails stuck to his sleeve. The brothers' makeshift weapons do not show a speck of any color other than red, as the gooey liquid drips from the silver utensils and the chair legs. Brad grabs Joey's shoulder and shakes it in a congratulatory gesture.

Then the brothers freeze. A low growl emanates from a shed in Mr. Wilson's backyard behind them. Joey and Brad eye each other quizzically, then slowly set their gazes on the small toolshed.

"That must be the final Howler," Joey says.

"We kill this one, and then it'll finally all be over," Brad replies.

"It's time to take back the night," Joey says, with a smirk.

Brad beholds the super blood moon now slowly descending behind the skyline as dawn approaches.

"You should do the honors, big bro," Joey says. "End it all. For all of us."

Brad nods once in appreciation for the monumental responsibility. "Should I have a speech ready? Like Neil Armstrong, when he stepped foot on the moon? Something that will live in infamy for all generations to recite when life gets hard?"

Joey scans the area. "We will be the only ones out here to hear it. Tell ya what. If you don't get killed and instead kill the last Howler, we can work on a rad saying together, then just tell everyone that's what you said when you did it."

"I like the way you think."

The Howler inside Mr. Wilson's shed growls louder, and the walls shake. The brothers hear tools clatter to the cement floor, then the beast turns its growl into a full-blown howl.

"Howlers doing what Howlers do best," Brad says. "It's time to silence the beast."

Joey nods. "I'll be right behind you."

The Bradshaw brothers inch down Mr. Wilson's driveway, past the returned Country Squire, and reach the shed, still gyrating, with howling sounds coming from within.

Brad grabs the metal door handle, nods once to his little brother behind him, and raises his knife-spear. Brad flings open the shed door and stumbles backward in shock and confusion.

The Howler wearing a yellow blouse, tire tracks across its belly and pants, stumbles forward with rage-filled eyes—eyes that Brad knows like the back of his hand, for they are twins with the woman he loves.

"Cheese and crackers! Is that Brenda?" Joey yells from behind Brad, breaking his brother from his paralysis.

The Brenda-Howler lunges forward, her snout dripping with blood.

"No, Joey. It's not Brenda. Not anymore."

Brad raises his knife-spear, but Brenda-Howler grabs his forearm with both paws and rips! Brad's arm comes clean off at the shoulder, showering himself and Brenda-Howler in blood. Brad screams as his knife-spear hits the driveway, and Joey stumbles backward in shock and disgust.

Brad looks at where his arm should be, at the tendons and veins dangling from the hole in his shoulder, like the mess of wires that connects their brand-new Nintendo and controllers to the television back at Brad's house. Bursts of red dots explode in his vision like fireworks, and a high-pitched ringing blooms in his ears. Brad knows he is seconds from passing out, both from blood loss and from seeing the wolf version of his girlfriend's twin sister rip his arm from its socket.

The Brenda-Howler scoops Brad's arm from the ground and slinks back into the shadows, cowering over the limb to munch on it, as if another beast might challenge her for the meal.

Thinking fast, Joey makes eye contact with his brother while removing Brad's shirt. "Look at me. Stay with me, Brad! We gotta get a tourniquet around this, or you're gonna bleed out. And fast!" Joey rips off Brad's shirt, noticing how little resistance Brad put up, like disrobing a mannequin made of goo. "Do not pass out on me!"

Brad somehow hears the slurping and chomping coming from the shadows through the ringing in his ears. He knows those sounds are of his girlfriend's sister feeding on his arm and hand. His stomach flips, and he wants to just disappear. To make it all go away. To pretend none of this is real.

Before Brad knows it, Joey removes Brad's shirt and ties it tight around the bloody stump at the end of his shoulder.

"This'll only buy you a little bit of time. We gotta get you to the hospital. Do you still have Mr. Wilson's keys?"

Brad sways, his eyes glazing over.

"Stay with me, big bro!" Joey retrieves Brad's dropped knife-spear from the ground and jams it into his back pocket, the wooden chair leg sticking up high enough to almost touch the back of Joey's head. He tucks his own fork-bayonet under an arm so he can use both hands to redirect Brad toward Mr. Wilson's car. Brad can only shuffle an inch at a time as Joey turns him, the soaked shirt tourniquet now dripping blood on the driveway.

Joey gets Brad safely to the passenger side of the car. "Where did you leave the keys?"

Brad pushes a pool of metallic-tasting saliva down his throat so he can croak out, "Kitchen table."

"Stay put. I'll be right back." Joey opens Brad's still-attached hand and slips the knife-spear into it. "In case she comes back."

Brad watches Joey sprint across the front lawn and into their parents' house to retrieve the keys to Mr. Wilson's car as the sounds of the Brenda-Howler munching on Brad's arm stops somewhere in the shadows behind him. Brad hears shifting and shuffling, like it is ready to emerge from its feast to finish him off. He darts his gaze toward his parents' front door, wondering how long it will take Joey to grab the keys and if it will be enough time to unlock the car doors before the Brenda-Howler rips the rest of his limbs from his body.

Brad refocuses on Mr. Wilson's backyard to his right and sees the Brenda-Howler shape lumbering toward him, snarling and growling. The sound of the front door opening and closing to his left makes Brad glance sideways toward his brother, sprinting across the lawn, keys dangling in hand.

Brad pans back to his right just as the Brenda-Howler's outstretched hands are a few feet from his face. He feels the puffs of air on his cheek coming from her nostrils and, without thought, swings the knife-spear at his girlfriend's sister's neck. The blade cuts through the furry but soft skin below its left ear, and Brad must listen to the scream of his girlfriend's twin, again from dying at his hand for the second time this weekend.

But the scream severs quickly—unlike when he ran her over with Mr. Wilson's car—and Brad watches the Brenda-Howler's furry, wrinkled, pointy-eared head lob through the air like a basketball at Joey, still running toward his brother and the car.

The Brenda-Howler's head hits the grass and rolls. Her snout acts like a Mongoose bike's kickstand, stopping the tumble right at Joey's feet.

Joey adjusts his thick-framed black glasses, grabs the fork-spear from his back pocket, and drives the tines into the Brenda-Howler's forehead. "Time to put a fork in you. You're done!"

Brad losing consciousness and slinking to the driveway against the car snaps Joey from his urge to concoct cheesy yet situation-appropriate one-liners. "I'm coming, big bro!" Joey digs his heels into the lawn, sidesteps around the decapitated final Howler's head, and rushes to the car.

After securing Brad inside the vehicle and getting into the driver's seat, Joey backs Mr. Wilson's car out of the driveway and points the car toward the Talbotsville emergency room. He pauses and rolls down the window to listen.

To listen for any growls or howls.

To listen to the silence.

"Hear anything?" Brad asks, then coughs and spits up a pool of blood.

"Just quiet."

Brad looks at Joey, his face paling from blood loss and his eyelids fluttering. "Yeah, Joey, we did it. We did it. We saved the town." Another round of coughing and wheezing racks his body. "We saved it all!"

"We certainly did, big brother."

Just as Joey is about to move his foot from the brake pedal to the accelerator, he hears a familiar and very distinct howl way in the distance. Joey eyes Brad to see if his brother heard the distinct Howler cry from what sounds like the next town over, negating any reason to celebrate.

Brad laughs so hard that he spits up another clump of blood all over the front of his shirt.

"What's so funny?" Joey asks, brows furrowed.

Brad forces one eye open to peer at his little brother. "Looks like the Howlers are now Parkview's problem."

A second howl comes from the direction of the neighboring city as Brad sits upright in a burst of adrenaline and realization. "I told Barbara to stay with her aunt in Parkview!"

And then a third distant howl, then a fourth, and a fifth, and a sixth, and a seventh…

Hiphopmcdougal

Brian Paone: Due to their current world tour, promoting their newest album, I had to catch the members of Hiphopmcdougal via conference call, while backstage, during their opening act's set at their sold-out show in Bolivia. Thank you, guys, for taking time to speak with me. I'll jump right in, as I'm sure you're trying to mentally and physically prepare for your show. How monumental was it to get a call from Director Sampson, requesting you to write a lyric-driven song for one of his films? And to know you paved the way for iconic theme songs to appear in horror films, such as "Cry Little Sister" from *Lost Boys*.

Julian Biggs: It was a pretty big deal. All we had really done at that point, that anyone may have heard, was a jingle for Pepperoni Tony's, and that song pretty much wrote itself, with a name like that.

Charlie Hodgson: Wally tracked us down through Pepperoni Tony's—that's what we all called him in town—and asked us what we could do for the project, and this felt way out of our league, but we couldn't say no. I mean, this was *the* Wally Sampson. His exploits were legendary. This was before the internet, so it was all just word-of-mouth stuff, but everything we had heard about him was creative, original, and absolutely bonkers.

Julian: We were pretty shocked to hear "Cry Little Sister" because it sounded almost exactly like "Howlers," but with a children's choir and completely different music. Honestly, we were just honored to be a part of the proud history of horror movie soundtracks.

BP: What inspired you to come up with a hip-hop/new-wave vibe, when, at the time, post-punk and glam bands were on the rise?

Charlie: Playing instruments is not really our thing. Now, drum machines and talking fast? Yeah, we're acing at that.

BP: Director Sampson originally only contracted you to write the theme song. How soon into recording the theme song "Howlers" did the music supervisor, Allison Castletop, ask you to create the film's entire score?

Charlie: Halfway through writing "Howlers," the original composer, Gareth Hernkey, suffered a terrible accident when he went out researching for this film. He went camping illegally in a wolf sanctuary and was eaten, and then subsequently fired.

Julian: So being the only other musicians—if you can call us that—on the project, Wally asked us to step up and to take a crack at it. It turns out scoring a scary movie isn't that hard. It's a lot of synthesizer and music that doesn't make people feel good, which we're actually pretty good at.

BP: Did you view the film before you wrote the score, or did Director Sampson just give you the script to work from?

Charlie: We spent a lot of time on set. We wanted to really get a feel for the movie, so Wally let us watch a lot of the filming and work on stuff as he made the movie, which was great. If you have a real clean copy of the VHS, you can catch us in the background of one of the shots at Landis Lake. It's pretty funny. I think Julian is actually holding his keytar.

Julian: It's about an hour and nine minutes in, right?

Charlie: Yeah, exactly. Sixty-nine minutes.

BP: Director Sampson digitally removed you guys from the 1997 special-edition DVD remaster. How do you feel about that?

Charlie: I mean, Wally, he's always tampering and tweaking things, and I don't think it's the original depiction of the film to take us out, but, if that's what Wally wants to do, that's what Wally gets.

BP: Did you record any unused music that did not make the film or the soundtrack, or how much of your score did Director Sampson reject and deem "unusable?"

Julian: We don't want to brag, but Wally loved us. We couldn't do anything wrong in his eyes. Or ears. So he never told us to change anything, which was great. He just made us feel super confident all the time.

Charlie: The only thing that got cut from the original film was a pretty intense piece we wrote for a scene where a man turns into a Howler, while using the bathroom. The whole scene winded up being too much for the final cut. It was something like fifteen minutes long. Wally insisted that it was filmed in real time, like imagining how long this guy would take to turn. It was like a really long scene, with a pretty expansive score—a lot of movements, if you know what I mean.

BP: Director Sampson has teased that he'll reinsert that scene into the director's cut that he keeps promising to release in theaters at some point. Do you think the fans will ever see that scene?

Charlie: I'm not sure, thirty-nine years later, that anyone is really ready for that scene. It's fifteen minutes long. Of a man. On a public toilet. Turning into a Howler. It's intense.

BP: How important was it for you to use the iconic line, "What's worse than werewolves?" as a soundbite in the theme song? Did Director Sampson give you any hardship with using any of his dialogue in a song that stayed at the top of the charts for over a year?

Charlie: Wally didn't mind us using that dialogue because it seemed to keep his film in the conversation for a little longer. We wanted to use some line from the film to punch up the song a bit. And we knew that particular line would become a classic. The delivery, the exchange, the whole tone was just perfect for setting up that chorus. There was another line from the bathroom scene that we loved, but we couldn't use that because it was cut.

Julian: Yeah, it was something about a courtesy flush, and some howling, and some screaming, and some more howling, and then a flush.

BP: Rumor has it that both of you are extras in the final climactic fight scene, dressed as Howlers. Fans have spent thirty-nine years guessing and debating which

Howlers you guys play. Can you finally put this argument to rest and tell us which Howlers?

Julian: I guess the thirty-ninth anniversary is the time to finally reveal this. During the scene when all the Howlers swarm the streets, there's a pretty clear shot of a Howler in a leather jacket that trips on a curb. And then the Howler behind him is looking around and doesn't see him, so he ends up falling over him. And they're both just rolling around on the sidewalk and trying to get up while still looking threatening. Do you remember that?

BP: [Nods]

Charlie: Yeah, well, we were the two Howlers to the left of them.

BP: One final question to wrap up this project and to end with a bang. I purposefully didn't ask any of the other interviewees because I know you guys would be the only ones who would tell me the unequivocal truth—the truth to the one thing over the past thirty-nine years that has plagued and smeared what should be a pristine legacy of this film. Without candy-coating anything, could you guys finally reveal why—

Charlie: Hold on, Brian…

[Unintelligible chatter from someone yelling at the band members]

Julian: Sorry, dude. We'll have to pick this up for the forty-first anniversary edition. Our intro music just started. It's showtime!

BP [Sighs, while hearing a few discernible notes of Beethoven's "Moonlight Sonata" over the phone, playing through the arena's house speakers, mixed with an uproar of applause and frantic cheering. Then the distinct and rapid *beep-beep-beep* to announce the call had ended.]

All cast members declined the invitation for an interview.

All emails, texts, social media messages, voicemails, faxes, certified letters through the postal service, and telegrams sent to Director Wally Sampson for an interview request went unanswered.

HOWLERS

A WOLF CRIED MEDIA PRODUCTION

JOEY BRADSHAW - CHAD WATERS
BRAD BRADSHAW - BOBO EASTMAN
BRAD BRADSHAW'S STUNT DOUBLE - ELLIOT PLATT
BRENDA REED & BARBARA REED - JENNIPHER JOHNS
MR. WILSON - HENRY P. STILLMAN
MR. WILSON'S STUNT DOUBLE - JAMES LEE
DR. PHYLLIS POTTINGER - MICHELLE BUTTS
SGT. AUTO VAN HELLSING - ALVIN CHAPMAN
SGT. AUTO VAN HELLSING'S STUNT DOUBLE - WILHELM HEULEN
MUSCLE MAN - PJ NILL
PUNK KID - CARL STOOPS
PUNK KID'S STUNT DOUBLE - MILLY HEESHAN
BABY FROM CRIB - LEANNE TEALOFT
BRENDA & BARBARA'S MOTHER - LAUREN SUMMERS
BRENDA & BARBARA'S FATHER - JASON XAVIER
GROSS OLD MAN - BOB GILROY
GRANDMOTHER OF DURAN DURAN FAN - MOLLY INDIGO
BLONDE GODDESS - ZOE WAN
LUNA - UNABLE TO DISCLOSE NAME DUE TO ACTORS GUILD VIOLATIONS
LUNA'S BOYFRIEND - BISHOP HERNANDEZ

HOWLER #1 - BROCK BELL
HOWLER #2 - JIMMY WELLZ
HOWLER #3 - CLINT YOUNGSTON
HOWLER #4 - WYNONA P. TAMLIN
HOWLER #5 - MATTHEW MOBELY
HOWLER #6 - GARRET YOUNG
DURAN DURAN-FAN HOWLER - BUNK PETERSON
ZEVON HOWLER - GREG GREGGERSON

DIRECTOR - WALLY SAMPSON
EXECUTIVE PRODUCER - FIONA WEST
ASSISTANT PRODUCER - ERIC DERRICK, PGA
EDITOR - LARRY WILSHIRE, ACE
ASSISTANT EDITOR - GENE CRANTON
SCREENWRITER - HAROLD H. DUNNY
DIRECTOR OF PHOTOGRAPHY - JUAN O'MALLEY
ASSISTANT DIRECTOR OF PHOTOGRAPHY - WILLY REED
SPECIAL FX SUPERVISOR - GREG BURGENSTEIN
ASSISTANT SPECIAL FX SUPERVISOR - VICTOR HAIL
SPECIAL FX DESIGNER - PATRICK ADLER
MAKEUP ARTIST - SANKEET KAPUR
SOUND ENGINEER - WILLIS WINSTON
ASSISTANT SOUND ENGINEER - EMILY DAVENPORT
FOLEY ARTIST - HECTOR SMITH
ASSISTANT FOLEY ARTIST - RAYFORD GRANSHIRE
FOLEY SUPERVISOR - GARY KNOLLBELL
FOLEY APPRENTICE - IAN LELAND

COSTUME DESIGNER - GABRIEL PUNCHWELL
ASSISTANT COSTUME DESIGNER - LAUREN LEAFBROOK
CAMERA OPERATOR - CLINT OFFERSON
CAMERA ASSISTANT - KARL BANKS
KEY GRIP - LOGAN CRUMP
SECONDARY GRIP - LARRY WATTS
CHIEF LIGHTING TECHNICIAN - HEIDI YAWNSON
BOOM OPERATOR - NELL SAN PABLO
GAFFER - JAMAL EARNFORD
STUNT COORDINATOR - KEN GUNNER
ASSISTANT STUNT COORDINATOR - STAN KIRK
SET DESIGNER - HECTOR L. XU
LOCATION SCOUT - GILBERT WRENSNEST III
ACCENT COACH - IGOR CROMWELL SMITH
CLAPPER - BILL BERGENSTEIN
ANIMAL HANDLERS - WONDERWOLVES INC
CRAFT SERVING - PD CATERING
MUSIC SUPERVISOR - ALLISON CASTLETOP
COMPOSER - H.H. MCDOUGAL